TURNABOUT

Also by Margaret Peterson Haddix

Just Ella

Among the Hidden

Leaving Fishers

Don't You Dare Read This, Mrs. Dunphrey

Running Out of Time

TURNABOUT

MARGARET PETERSON HADDIX

ALADDIN PAPERBACKS
New York London Toronto Sydney Singapore

First Aladdin Paperbacks edition May 2002
Copyright (c) 2000 by Margaret Peterson Haddix

Aladdin Paperbacks
An imprint of Simon & Schuster Children's Publishing Division
1230 Avenue of the Americas New York, NY 10020

Designed by Steve Scott
The text of this book was set in Melior.
Manufactured in the United States of America

20 19 18 17 16 15 14 13

The Library of Congress has cataloged the hardcover edition of this book as follows:
Haddix, Margaret Peterson. Turnabout / Margaret Peterson Haddix.
p. cm.
Summary: After secretly receiving injections at the age of 100 that are meant to reverse the aging process, Melly and Anny Beth grow younger until, as teenagers, they try to find a guardian to take care of them as they return to infancy.
ISBN-13: 978-0-689-82187-5 (hc)
ISBN-10: 0-689-82187-5 (hc)
[1. Science fiction.] I. Title
pz7.H11135 Tu 2000
[Fic]-dc21 99-086677
ISBN-13: 978-0-689-84037-1 (Aladdin pbk.)
ISBN-10: 0-689-84037-3 (Aladdin pbk.)

For Mary Greshel and Lacie Tucker,
and in memory of Opal Haddix

With thanks to my grandmother Mary Greshel; my husband's grandmother Lacie Tucker; and my friend Margot McVoy for indulging my hypothetical questions and for telling me what it was like to live through much more of the twentieth century than I personally experienced. Thanks also to Renee Cho and David Gale for their help with this book and many others.

TURNABOUT

PART ONE

PART ONE

April 21, 2085

My sixteenth birthday. Sad, sad day. What I mind most—what I've been dreading most—is losing my license. I could still pass for being older for at least another year or two, but the agency won't let me. Against the rules, they say. We know best, they say. How can they be so sure when this is all new territory?

At least Anny Beth can still drive, since she's only eighteen. I don't know what I'd do without Anny Beth. I don't know what we'll do when she hits sixteen. And beyond that . . .

The agency lady called this morning to make sure I was ready for her annual visit. She said, "You still seem to be holding up."

I said, "I don't like the other choices."

She didn't laugh, the way I meant her to.

I told her my Memory Book was done, and she said, "It's not easy, is it?"

How do you answer a question like that?

My body feels good. Healthy. Teeming with life and possibility. I remember this feeling from the last time. I had such hope for the future then.

It's not the same when my body feels hopeful and my mind knows that the future is only sixteen more years of loss.

"Do you want to be younger?" someone asked her.

Amelia Lenore Hazelwood roused herself from the half slumber she lived in most of the time. She squinted through cataract-covered eyes at the trio of white-coated people at the foot of her bed, and debated whether they were really there or just apparitions from one of her dreams. Even at this point, so near the end, she hated the thought of becoming one of those old ladies who talk to nothing. But most of her dreams were about Roy and the farm, or her children when they were babies and toddlers—instead of gray-haired grandparents she barely recognized. None of her dreams involved white coats. She adjusted her hearing aid.

"What's that?" she said.

A man stepped forward, and she was glad, because men were easier to hear. Something about the pitch of their voices, the doctor had explained. She thought it was because she had spent her life listening to men. Roy had always wanted to tell her what to do, and now her sons and the doctors were in charge. . . .

"I said, would you like to be younger?" the man said, enunciating very carefully, as though she were witless as well as hard of hearing.

Or maybe he was witless. It was a mighty stupid

question to ask a woman who was almost a whole year past her one hundredth birthday.

"Sure," she mumbled, because he seemed to expect an affirmative answer. It took too much energy to do things people didn't expect. She started closing her eyes again, having lost interest in the conversation.

"No, wait," he said, springing forward and taking her hand.

Few enough people touched her in the nursing home that she kept her eyes halfway open. But she stared unseeingly and didn't bother telling him that she couldn't hear what he said next. Then a woman stepped forward and droned on for a while, her voice as high-pitched and indecipherable as a mosquito's buzz. When she finished, the other man spoke, his voice the rumble of thunder on a summer afternoon. At last the woman thrust a pen and a sheaf of papers at Amelia and pointed, clearly expecting her to sign.

Feebly, Amelia moved the papers closer and farther from her eyes until she could focus on a line at the bottom. The smudge of small print above the line would have been illegible to Amelia even a decade earlier. She looked up at the expectant faces around her. Then she took the pen and signed with a flourish, admiring the loops of the *A* and *L* and *H*. She'd lost just about every other skill—even the basic ones, like being able to feed herself. But she was still capable of producing the copperplate signature she'd learned almost a century ago. It was the one thing she had left to be vain about.

The white-coated crew all grinned, and the two men did high fives off to the side, evidently not realizing that her vision was best out of the corners of her eyes. For a second she wondered if she'd just signed away all her savings, what little there were, or fallen for some other scam. But she was pretty sure her signature wasn't binding anymore. She was too old. She was almost dead. Surely someone had mentioned something about one of her sons, Dick or George, having power of attorney for her, being her legal guardian, whatever it was called. Surely it didn't matter what she had signed.

April 21, 2085

Melly placed her journal back on the shelf beside the others and all the Memory Books. It made quite an impressive display, a wallful of books, 168 altogether. But she rarely thought of them that way— they were 84 and 84, always separate. Anny Beth had no such system. She chucked everything into some cardboard box in the storage shed. That is, if she bothered to make a book at all. As she'd told one of the more persistent agency ladies, "Honey, if you'd lived a life like mine, you'd understand— some years you're happy to forget."

Impulsively, Melly pulled down one of the closest Memory Books and opened it at random: *Neddy had the croup all winter, seemed like. I spent so much time holding him over the steam that I felt like I would evaporate too. . . .*

She skipped back a few pages: *The corn crop failed in September. . . .*

Not long after came the words Melly knew were there: *Neddy died on November 18.*

Melly felt no more pain than if she'd read of someone else's tragedy. It was another lifetime. It might as well be someone else's life. Maybe Anny Beth was right, and they were better off forgetting. But Melly, for one, found the Memory Books comforting. She slipped the book back into place and remembered a briefing session on rituals that the agency had sponsored. Early on, the agency had been very big on briefings. At the session about rituals a peppy blond woman who looked to be all of twenty-two had stood in front of the rows of wheelchairs and practically cheered, "Rituals are good! They remind us we're alive!"

Anny Beth had leaned over to Melly and muttered in a stage whisper everyone could hear, "I'm out of here."

Then she'd wheeled herself away.

But Melly had stayed. Back then she'd still had happy memories of family meals and family holidays and family rituals that got six kids and a husband off to school and work each morning with minimal hassle. And back then she'd still been interested in what the agency had to say.

Now she heard the doorbell ring downstairs.

"Melly! Agency lady's here!" Anny Beth shouted up.

They passed each other on the stairs.

"I may need your help later," Melly murmured.

"Shame I don't still have my papaw's hunting rifle," Anny Beth replied.

Melly shook her head. "You know what I mean," she said.

"Yeah," Anny Beth said, serious for once. "Call in the reinforcements whenever you want. I'll be ready."

Anny Beth went on up to her room, and Melly

got the door. She put on a smile for the matronly-looking woman with blunt-cut hair and sensible shoes. They always wore sensible shoes—which was strange, given how insensible the agency had been.

"Well," the woman said pointlessly. "It's that time again."

"Yes," Melly said.

She held the door open, and as the woman brushed past her Melly saw the contrast between the woman's blocky, middle-aged form and Melly's trim, blue-jeans-clad figure. Melly's stomach showed, flat and perfect, in the three-inch gap between her cropped T-shirt and the hip-hugging jeans. It shouldn't have mattered, but Melly still felt a shot of triumph, *I'm younger than you!* Actually, nothing could have been further from the truth, but sometimes even Melly forgot.

"Can I get you something to drink, Mrs. . . . er, Miss . . . er, Ms., uh—"

"Ms. Simmons," the woman said with a look that made Melly feel like a kid playing house while her parents were away. There was no reason for that feeling, but Melly had been getting it more and more lately. "Nothing to drink, thanks."

They sat in the living room, and Ms. Simmons started Melly through the usual routine. Touch your nose. Raise your hand when you hear a beep. Look up, look down, follow the light on the wall. Jump up and down, and then let's check your heart rate. Just one more vial of blood—and then could you urinate into a jar, please?

Melly went through the paces as stoically as a lab rat. After more than two hours the woman finally checked off the last box on her form.

"We won't know for sure until the blood and urine tests are back, of course, but you certainly seem to be an absolutely normal, healthy sixteen-year-old," the woman said.

Melly shrugged. This wasn't news.

"Now, about puberty—," the woman began.

"I'll lose my period in about a year," Melly started, because she'd rather say it herself than listen to Ms. Simmons stumble through. "My breasts will shrink. My pubic hair will disappear. I'll stop having to shave under my arms. Anything else?"

"Your hips will, uh, you know. Smooth out." The woman was clearly embarrassed. Melly decided Ms. Simmons had probably never had kids, never had to discuss the birds and bees with anyone under twenty. "You'll shrink and lose weight. And then there are the emotional changes—"

Melly nodded. She decided to break one of Anny Beth's cardinal rules: Never ask the agency anything. They can't help.

"What have the others found?" Melly asked. "Are things pretty normal? I mean, I guess *normal* isn't the right word. Is it like the first time?"

"Basically. I'm sure you can handle it," the woman said, gathering up her papers. Once they were all in a neat stack, she looked directly at Melly again. "There's one more thing. I believe the agency has been most understanding of your desire for independence. But surely you realize—you're sixteen now. You can't live on your own."

Melly struggled to sound calm and reasonable. "I'm not on my own. Anny Beth and I—"

Ms. Simmons shook her head impatiently. When she answered, Melly could tell she wasn't even trying to sound calm and reasonable. "You're a couple of kids now. What are you going to do when some busybody neighbor decides to call the authorities? What would you say?"

"What we've been saying for the past two years. We're orphans. That's true enough, isn't it? My big sister, Anny Beth, is taking care of me while she works and goes to school—"

Ms. Simmons was frowning and shaking her head. "That will work for another year, tops. Then you'll have truant officers after you—"

"I'm home-schooled."

Ms. Simmons raised an eyebrow in disgust. "Uh-huh. Right. Can't you face facts? I'm truly sorry—I do admire what you've tried to do. But you're going to have to come back."

"Never," Melly whispered.

They came in on stretchers, in wheelchairs, and on walkers. One or two of the heartier souls held only a cane. Amelia, who was back in a wheelchair for the first time in more than a year, noticed with a jolt that even the stretcher set looked lively. She folded her hands in her lap and waited.

A tall, gangly man bounded to the front of the unfamiliar conference room.

"All of you know me, I think—I'm Dr. Reed, and I have wonderful news for you all today. My partner, Dr. Jimson, will be showing the slides—"

On cue, the room lights dimmed and a screen beside Dr. Reed lit up. The picture reminded Amelia of a string of beads.

"This is a magnified sample from Mr. Royal, I believe, but all of you are showing the same results: Your telomeres are growing!"

Fifty pairs of eyes watched him blankly in the near dark. He shrugged apologetically. "I know, I know, that's technicalese. Probably none of you even knew you had telomeres."

"That's true," a man in the front grunted.

"Telomeres are, most simply, strings on the end of your chromosomes. You can think of them as a repeated sequence of beads on a necklace." Amelia felt proud of herself for noticing the resemblance.

She listened a little more intently as Dr. Reed continued. "Scientists have known since the 1970s that each time a normal cell divides, the repeated sequences are reduced. It's like the necklace shrinks. Until very recently it was believed that only abnormal cells, like cancer cells, were immortal and didn't have shrinking telomeres."

A woman gasped. "We have cancer!"

Dr. Reed looked impatient. "No, no, it's not that. You're all perfectly healthy. Better than perfectly healthy. That's what I'm trying to tell you. A cancer cell's telomeres don't grow like this. The growing telomeres mean you're all getting younger. You are, to coin a phrase, unaging!"

He stepped back with a triumphant glow on his face, waiting for his news to sink in. For a moment there was dead silence in the room, then everyone began to buzz: "What's he mean?" "How can someone unage?" "Did he say what I thought he said?"

A woman two chairs down from Amelia raised her hand and asked in a querulous voice, "How come our families don't visit us anymore?"

The triumphant look slipped from Dr. Reed's face. "W-e-ell, that's something I need to talk to all of you about. In fact, I've wanted to bring this up for a while. Dr. Jimson, could you join me?"

The lights came back on full strength, and everyone blinked at their harshness. Once Amelia's pupils had adjusted, she saw a slender woman in a white coat walking up the aisle. Amelia knew she'd seen her before. Dr. Jimson had small, wire-rimmed glasses and precisely clipped black hair—the perfect bob Amelia and all her friends had been scandalized by and secretly longed for back when they were young women.

Dr. Reed and Dr. Jimson looked at each other, both obviously waiting for the other to speak. Finally Dr. Jimson cleared her throat.

"The reason your families don't visit you anymore," she started in a surprisingly soft voice, "is that they think you're dead."

Dr. Reed held up his hand, as if anticipating protests. "We didn't plan to do things this way, but it might help. Please—"

Everyone had begun to talk at once. Dr. Reed's voice got louder. "Please hear me out. Your families all thought you were dead because, for a week or so, you appeared to be dead. You all went into—well, let's call it a coma, for lack of a better word. Dr. Jimson and I have never seen anything like it, and we're still doing computer searches to see if we can find any record of anything similar. You and your families signed documents to let us do extensive research on your bodies, because of the experiment, so we kept you all together—"

For a fleeting moment Amelia wondered if she

really had died. This was not at all how she had pictured heaven, but things had been so strange lately, maybe it was. Why, she could kick off her bed covers at night now. She could rise up on her arms once again and look out the window. Maybe heaven was only about small improvements.

Around her everyone started to grumble at once: "I never signed anything!" "Documents? What documents?" "I said I'd give my body to science after I died, not before!"

Dr. Reed reached behind him for a thick notebook. "Your waivers are all in here. You may inspect your signatures afterward if you want." His voice carried a chill in it. "Some of you begged me to be involved in this experiment."

The grumbling grew louder. "I don't remember begging!" "Doctors!"

Dr. Jimson stepped forward.

"Please," she said. "I know this isn't an easy situation to grasp. The fifty of you are pioneers of sorts, and Dr. Reed and I aren't entirely sure how to handle things either." Dr. Reed flashed her a look of scorn, evidently for revealing any weakness or uncertainty. But the crowd quieted down. "I think it's best if you let us explain the situation fully, and then we can talk about what to do."

She waited for total silence. Dr. Reed started to speak, but she flashed him a look that shut him up too.

"All of you are participants in Project Turnabout," Dr. Jimson continued. "We explained the experiment when we got your permission—and we did get your permission, though many of you apparently don't remember it now. Given the changes your bodies have been through, it would be perfectly understandable if you have some short-term amnesia. We'll be testing for that." She paused. Everyone waited. "Now, about your families. They know that your bodies were to be donated to science, but they weren't given all the details. Between the fifty of you, you have something like a thousand descendants, and this is a secret project for reasons you, most of all, should understand. So, initially at least, we didn't feel we could let them know everything. And, um, we're still not sure about the final outcome, so we didn't think it was fair to anyone to make your families grieve twice."

With a grasp of subtlety she thought she'd lost, Amelia realized what Dr. Jimson meant: They still might die soon. Even after their miraculous revivals. Even with their longer telomeres, whatever those were.

A man in the back raised his hand. "I guess you don't want other scientists knowing what you're doing afore you get your Nobel Prize or whatever. I can see that," he drawled slowly. "But my boys are factory workers. They ain't a-gonna tell no one. It don't seem fair. . . ."

MARGARET PETERSON HADDIX

Dr. Reed gave Dr. Jimson a let-me-handle-this-one look. She stepped aside.

"Mr. Seaver," he called to a man not far down the row from Amelia. "Where does your son work?"

"TV station down in Cincinnati," he said.

Dr. Reed nodded. "And Mrs. Burn-Jones, what about your grandson Eddy?"

"The *National Enquirer*," she muttered.

Some people snickered. Dr. Reed smirked.

"You all have been in nursing homes for a while—some of you for a dozen years or more. But you remember tabloids, don't you? Can't you picture the headlines? 'Ninety-year-olds Drink from Fountain of Youth,' 'Nursing Home Patients Gain Immortality'—the media wouldn't leave you alone. You'd have to live like freaks in a circus. We keep this secret, you can have normal lives."

Amelia wondered how he could say that so confidently. She'd had a normal life, and she'd pretty much finished it. Normal life ended in death. What was he doing talking about immortality?

"Is that what's going to happen?" someone else asked. "Are we immortal now?" Amelia thought she heard equal measures of fear and hope in his voice, but perhaps that was only what she felt.

"We don't know. You're still susceptible to accident or disease, but it's very unlikely now that you'll die of old age. The injections we gave you, a formula we're calling PT-1, caused laboratory animals to live indefinitely, and in much more youthful states. We took very old rats, gave them the shots, and then gave them more shots when they unaged to about middle age. We think we can keep them at the rat equivalent of twenty-five or thirty practically forever. And that's what I've been trying to tell you, before you all got distracted. You're going to be able to walk again. You're going to be able to see well again. You're going to be able to hear. I don't know about immortality, but I can promise you this: You're all going to be young again."

All the patients began to talk at once again, and the doctors made no attempt to stop them. Then a quivery voice somehow floated above the noise:

> "Dem bones, dem bones gonna
> Walk around. . . ."

One by one, everyone else stopped talking and listened to the eerie voice.

> "Dem bones, dem bones gonna
> Walk around.
> Dem bones, dem bones gonna
> Walk around. . . ."

Suddenly recognizing the song, Amelia wanted to giggle. If she were younger, she thought, she'd have half a mind to join in. Then she remembered:

She was younger. Her voice cracking, she sang along on the last line:

"Hear the word of the Lord."

From their blank expressions Amelia could tell the doctors had spent more of their childhoods in science classes than at Sunday school. She glanced back at the woman who'd been singing: Her shrunken face was a mask of wrinkles, and a tiny smile was the only evidence that she'd said anything at all. Amelia decided the explaining was up to her.

"It's from the Bible," she said. "Ezekiel. He was a crazy prophet in the wilderness, and God showed him a pile of bones and told him, 'I can make them all come to life again.' And Ezekiel prophesied, and what God said happened. The bones all joined together into skeletons and got bodies and skin and hair and everything, and stood up and were alive again."

"Then what?" Dr. Reed asked. He'd gone a little pale. "What happened next?"

Amelia thought about it.

"I don't remember exactly," she said. "I think Ezekiel just starts talking about the fate of Israel."

Somehow it had never occurred to her to wonder how the skeletons felt about being brought back to life.

A woman in the back suddenly hollered out, "This is against the will of God! You've denied me my entrance to heaven!"

"No, no, we never—we wanted . . . ," Dr. Reed started to explain. But he had to stop to mop sweat from his brow.

Over the hubbub the same voice that had sung rang out again, "Aw, come on, Louise. How do you know they haven't saved you from hell?"

Then it was hopeless, the doctors had no chance of getting anyone's attention again. Amelia saw Dr. Reed lean over and whisper to Dr. Jimson. Amelia thought she could see well enough again to read his lips—he said, "Get them out of here!"

As Amelia's chair was being pushed out of the room, she passed the stretcher of the woman who'd sung. The woman turned her head and grinned at Amelia. "I'm Anny Beth Flick," she said. "Don't you just love to see people all riled up?"

April 21, 2085

Melly and Anny Beth went out dancing to celebrate Melly's birthday. They hardly needed any excuse for dancing anymore. It was like some rhythm sang in their bones all the time, secretly urging, "Dance. Run. Move. Get going!" Melly went jogging every morning now, and Anny Beth did aerobics three or four nights a week, but somehow that wasn't enough. They'd talked about it; neither one of them remembered the dancing urge being quite so powerful the first time.

"But there were always chores then," Melly had said. "All those buckets of water I had to lug up the hill . . . all the grain we thrashed by hand . . . I used to fall into bed too worn out even to sleep."

"Not me," Anny Beth had said, with her usual ornery grin. "I always had energy at night."

Melly had playfully slugged her.

They were acting more like kids now. Melly knew that. She thought about Ms. Simmons's pursed lips and knew how she'd view Melly and Anny Beth's behavior. But what was she going to say—"Act your age"? Which age?

They stepped into the dance club now, their silver boots gleaming in the strobe lights. The crowd in front of them was a blur of tie-dye, neon polyester, and smiley-face prints. Melly figured that this was about the fifth time in her life that the fashions of the 1970s were "in." What was so enduring about all those psychedelic daisies that they kept coming back? This time, though, the look always had to be paired with what Anny Beth called "futuristic Reynolds Wrap." No one else in the dance club remembered foil, of course, since aluminum had been mined out years ago. Melly caught a glimpse of herself in the mirrored walls. With her short, fitted silver dress and glittery eye shadow and multi-colored hair, she looked just like a "Predictions of the Future" fashion display she'd seen several decades ago. Had the fashion futurists been so wise that they knew what was coming, or had these fashions come into style simply because that was what people predicted? Were all successful prophecies self-fulfilling?

Melly thought about sharing her musings with Anny Beth, but decided against it. "What are you doing, thinking again?" Anny Beth would say. "It's your birthday. We're at a club. Dance."

It was too loud to talk anyhow. Melly threw herself into the music, jerking her limbs alongside dozens of other anonymous bodies.

Hours later Anny Beth leaned over and shouted in Melly's ear. "—eat?" was all Melly caught. Melly nodded. They went to a restaurant next door and ordered the largest platters of burgers and fries available. Melly's ears were still ringing when their food arrived.

MARGARET PETERSON HADDIX

"If I really were a teenager with decades ahead of me, I would *not* be ruining my ears like that," Melly said. "I can't believe what those kids do."

"Oh, don't be such an old lady," Anny Beth said. "Irresponsibility is what adolescence is all about."

Melly snorted. "Which psychology book did you read that one in?"

That had been one of their latest projects, reading about adolescence so that they could blend in better. They'd mostly found the books hilarious, as if describing a species of animal they'd never encountered. Each of them had been a teenager before, each of them had raised teenagers—but they'd never seen anyone act like the books said all teenagers behaved.

Anny Beth paused to smile suggestively at a guy a few booths away. He smiled back but didn't approach. Melly wondered how she and Anny Beth could look and act so much like typical teenagers, but still give off such forbidding vibes.

A camera crew walked up the aisle and stopped beside the guy Anny Beth had smiled at. "And now," one of the men in the crew said dramatically into a microphone, "more about Peter's life! We'll follow him all night long! See every second of his existence!"

Peter beamed into the camera.

Anny Beth rolled her eyes. "Just another publicity hound."

Melly counted the other camera crews in the restaurant—there were ten in sight, and probably at least that many out of her view.

"Isn't everyone a publicity hound now?" Melly asked.

"No," Anny Beth said. "Not you and me."

Melly shook her head and tried to remember when she had first noticed people becoming such exhibitionists. She'd heard of people having their own Web sites back in the early years of the twenty-first century, where they kept cameras trained on themselves twenty-four hours a day. But that had been a rare occurrence; back then, even celebrities had tried to avoid the cameras sometimes. Nowadays everyone seemed to want to reveal everything about themselves to the entire world, and modern technology had practically made that possible. It made no sense to Melly, because the extreme exposure often got people in trouble. The police had only to scroll the public-access video sites to catch criminals; divorce courts never had to prove adultery, because it was always on tape. Melly shivered thinking about what her and Anny Beth's lives would be like if their secret were ever exposed. They'd never have a moment's peace.

Anny Beth lost interest in the camera crew. "So," she said. "It's your birthday. Sweet sixteen and never been kissed."

It was an old-fashioned saying, one Melly hadn't heard in years. Unbidden, tears sprang to her eyes as she remembered all the kisses she'd be forgetting now. She and Roy had started dating when she was fifteen. They'd exchanged their first shy kisses under the apple tree on Roy's father's farm the day he proposed. . . .

"Don't do that," Anny Beth pleaded. "I'm sorry. I can't take you getting mushy on me."

Melly brushed the tears away and grimaced. "Do you ever regret not volunteering for the Cure?" she asked.

"You mean, do I wish I were dead? Of course not."

"Maybe it would have worked for us—"

Anny Beth made a face. "I doubt it. And it wasn't worth the risk to find out. Is this birthday getting to you? Remember—you've got a lot of good life ahead of you. At least, I do, and I want you to keep me company in it."

Melly couldn't help smiling at Anny Beth's mocking selfishness. But she couldn't match Anny Beth's banter. "Maybe the agency's right," she said.

"Them? Never," Anny Beth said reflexively. She took a huge bite of hamburger, sucking in a dangling strand of onion like someone reeling in a fishing line.

"No, really," Melly said. "What are we going to do when—you know. When you can't drive anymore.

When we get too short to reach the top cabinets in the kitchen. When we forget how to tie our shoes. When I'm back in diapers—" She was whispering now, partly because she didn't want anyone to overhear, and partly because the tears were threatening to come back.

"First of all, start taking the bus," Anny Beth said, chewing on the onion. "Use the step stool. Wear Velcro shoes."

"And the other?" Melly spoke so softly she knew Anny Beth couldn't hear her. But Anny Beth knew what she meant.

"That's years away. You were potty trained pretty young, weren't you?"

Melly grimaced and didn't answer.

Anny Beth placed her hamburger down on her plate with unusual care. "Look, I know it's not going to be easy. But it's not worth ruining our lives now with fretting. We'll worry about that when the time comes. We'll think of something. I assure you, I have no intention of going back to any sort of institution. I lost too much of the other end of my life in one of them places."

Melly always knew Anny Beth was totally serious when she slipped back into bad grammar. It was sort of comforting. But Melly refused to be comforted. "Fine," she said. "You fiddle while Rome burns. I'm going to find someone to take care of us."

"Tonight?" Anny Beth asked.

"Soon," Melly said. She hated it when Anny Beth deflated her grand pronouncements.

"Shouldn't it be 'fiddle while Rome unburns'?" Anny Beth asked. "Because that's pretty much what we're doing. Ever watch a fire video on rewind? It's really awesome to see a house put itself back together. . . ."

Melly let Anny Beth's chatter envelop her like a cocoon. Anny Beth was probably right—she should just enjoy herself tonight. But tomorrow—she'd start her search tomorrow.

Amelia rolled her chair up to the dinner table in her usual spot beside Mrs. Flick. The fifty Project Turnabout volunteers had been at the agency for three months now, and they'd broken down into cliques just like kids at school. It hadn't happened that way at Amelia's old nursing home, because there was always someone new arriving or someone old dying. But no one had died at the agency. And they certainly never saw anyone new. Just the same handful of nurses and doctors and aides. It reminded Amelia of growing up in the hills of Kentucky. She could remember only two or three times in her entire childhood when she'd met an outsider.

But there had been no one like Mrs. Flick around when Amelia was growing up.

Amelia wasn't quite sure why she and Mrs. Flick had hit it off. If the agency had been a school, Mrs. Flick would have been the unofficial leader and class clown and Most Likely to Get Into Trouble all at once. She was the one everyone else talked about—or would have, except that she herself liked to do most of the talking. And somehow she always knew everything that was going on. She was off the stretcher now and in a wheelchair once more, but still—how did the wheelchair make her so mobile that she seemed to know what Dr. Reed and Dr. Jimson were thinking before they knew themselves?

"You hear what the meeting's about tonight?" Amelia asked, leaning back while the attendant placed a plate of food in front of her.

"Our families. Again," Mrs. Flick said, her eyes rolled skyward in disdain. At 102, she was the oldest at the agency but somehow managed to seem the most youthful.

"I miss my Morty and Angeline," Mrs. Swanson whined across the table. "Why, oh, why won't they let me see them?"

Mrs. Swanson was afflicted with a flair for melodrama.

"Nobody's stopping you, toots," Mrs. Flick shot back. "There's a pay phone in the hallway. Why don't you use it?"

Amelia decided to stay out of the discussion. She took a bite of her chicken à la king.

"But they don't want us to contact our families," Mrs. Swanson said with a sniff. "I don't know how you were raised"—the look down her nose made it clear she had some definite ideas—"but I have always shown proper respect for authority. After they've been so kind as to save our lives, I believe it's my duty to—"

"Oh, stow it, Louise," Mrs. Flick said in disgust. "They don't know what they want. They're fighting among themselves too."

Chewing a particularly stringy piece of chicken, Amelia wondered if Mrs. Flick was right. Certainly Dr. Reed and Dr. Jimson had been nothing but cordial to each other in public, but they mostly seemed to contrive to be at opposite sides of the room at every meeting. For a pair that had just orchestrated a scientific miracle, neither one of them seemed particularly happy.

Amelia swallowed her chicken carefully. "What about you?" she asked Mrs. Flick. "Why aren't you in on the fight?"

"Yeah," Mrs. Swanson contributed. "If anyone was gonna call from that pay phone, it'd be you—"

"Maybe I just don't care about seeing my family," Mrs. Flick said defiantly. "Ever think of that?"

Amelia and Mrs. Swanson exchanged glances. Amelia was willing to let it lie, but not Mrs. Swanson.

"Well, why ever not? You have family, don't you?"

"Sure," Mrs. Flick said. "Five kids, fourteen grandkids, and a passel of greats. Only, I raised every single one of them wrong. The ones who ain't dead are in jail—or should be."

Mrs. Swanson wasn't going to let it go. "Surely one or two of them—"

"Nope," Mrs. Flick said cavalierly. Amelia wondered if Mrs. Swanson saw the glitter of pain in Mrs.

MARGARET PETERSON HADDIX

Flick's eyes. "They're reprobates and blackguards through and through."

"My word. Anny Beth Flick, you ought to be ashamed of yourself. Why, a woman's family is her crowning glory, which is why I worked so hard on Morty and Angeline—"

"Louise," Amelia said. "Shut up."

There was a shocked silence. Even Amelia couldn't quite believe what she'd said.

Then, "Well," Mrs. Swanson sniffed. "I know when I'm not wanted." She jerked her chair back from the table and walked away. She was probably the best walker in the group. Amelia could hear her muttering as she left, "My word, such rudeness. You'd think if they were going to grant immortality, they'd have screened people a little more closely. . . ."

"My view exactly," Mrs. Flick hollered after her. "How'd you get in?"

Amelia went back to eating docilely, just a little old lady minding her own business. She didn't look at Mrs. Flick.

"Thanks," Mrs. Flick murmured. "Thanks for sticking up for me. Not many people have done that in my life."

Amelia shrugged. "You stick up for yourself well enough," she said.

"Yeah." Mrs. Flick grinned, and for a second Amelia could see past the wrinkles and picture how she must have been as a kid: eyes full of mischief, probably pigtails perpetually askew, a streak of mud across her cheek. Some things didn't change with age, and orneriness was one of them. But now, if the doctors were right, Mrs. Flick would get the chance to be a kid again. Or, not a kid, Amelia reminded herself, but middle-aged, which sounded plenty young to her. Even after six months the idea still took some getting used to. Amelia kept waiting for the doctors to discover a catch. So far, the only thing was she couldn't remember the last few months before the first injection of PT-1. But the doctors still said that was nothing to worry about, that the memory was bound to come back. And even if it didn't, what was there to remember of any worth?

"It makes you wonder, though, don't it?" Mrs. Flick asked.

"Excuse me?" Amelia said, wondering what she'd missed.

"How did they pick us? Why didn't they get them some ex-presidents? Or geniuses—you know, real important people?"

Amelia had noticed that everyone at the agency seemed dead ordinary. "Do you see fifty ex-presidents lying around in nursing homes? We were handy. Convenient. And don't you remember what Dr. Reed said at that last meeting—that PT-1 will probably never be offered to the whole world, just selected people who have earned the right to live forever. So we should be grateful—"

Mrs. Flick shook her head. "This ain't going to the Mother Teresas of the world. Can't you see how people are gonna fight over it? Dr. Reed and Dr. Jimson, they're on the verge of starting World War III. But you know how it's all going to end up. Same way as everything else. The people who can pay will get what they want. Only, bet you anything it won't be legal. They'll have to pay in dark alleys— and maybe get their throats slit trying to live forever. This here thing's a curse."

"Not for us," Amelia said.

"We don't really know that yet, do we?" The grin broke out again. "But hot-dang, I do like trying to figure out what's going to happen next around here!"

Amelia looked around at the rows of gray and white heads bent over their dinners. People didn't seem ecstatic at the thought of living forever. They seemed mostly confused. What exactly would it mean to live in middle age for as long as anyone could imagine? What would they do with all that time?

Dr. Jimson had begun hinting that maybe they should stop thinking so much about their families— "the families from the life where you aged," as she put it—and realize that they would probably marry again, have more kids. But Amelia wondered:

Unless their kids got PT-1 too, wouldn't it be strange for them to someday be older than their parents? And who would she marry? There were only fifteen men in Project Turnabout, and she couldn't imagine marrying any of them. Anyone else would grow old on her, always traveling the other direction in time.

All the complications gave her a headache. It made her want to pick up the phone and call one of her sons, ask him to solve her problems for her. It'd been kind of nice doing that the last few years. But had she relied on them too much—so much that they were relieved when they heard she was dead? Had they seen her only as a burden toward the end? She'd seen herself that way.

Amelia closed her eyes for a moment, more befuddled than ever. She did long to call her family. Now that Mrs. Flick had planted the notion of just rolling right up to the pay phone in the lobby, she wanted to do that. She wanted to find out if her three surviving children were still doing okay, if her granddaughter's breast cancer had gone into remission, if her newest great-great-grandchild, the one with the funny name—Lakota? Shoshone? Something Indian—was walking yet. But if she had been just a burden, would they really want to hear from her? Should she wait until she was more independent again—walking on her own, able to live on her own, maybe even—good grief!—working?

She wished she'd been able to see her funeral. Then she could have understood what she meant to people. Somehow, she realized, she had always expected to be able to watch everyone's reactions at her funeral, see who cried and how hard. Sure, she'd expected to be dead before her funeral, but she did believe in an afterlife. And her view of heaven always included the ability to spy on Earth. She never expected to find herself still alive, but dead to her family.

"Want that?"

Amelia opened her eyes, realized that Mrs. Flick was pointing her fork at the slice of apple pie to the left of Amelia's plate.

"No," Amelia murmured. "You can have it."

"Thanks." Mrs. Flick beamed and slid the plate across the table. She dug in with relish.

Watching her friend, Amelia suddenly envied Mrs. Flick's lack of attachments. In the midst of all the confusion, one thing was sure: Mrs. Flick was going to enjoy her second chance at life.

April 22, 2085

Melly sharpened a pencil. Pencils were antiques now, and had been ever since erasable ink had finally been perfected sixty years ago. And of course computers made even pens pretty much unnecessary. But pencils helped her to think; her brain needed the physical act of turning the sharpener handle, the smell of wood chips and lead, the sight of the pencil point against the white paper. And today she needed all the help she could get.

Her pencil taken care of, she switched on the computer.

"Um, something about families looking for kids to adopt. Nice families," she told the computer. Even though she knew it was ridiculous, she hoped the computer didn't hear the note of anxiety in her voice. This was an old model—she got it five years ago when she was pretending to go to college—but it still had the obligatory emotion sensor. She and Anny Beth joked that computers had become so human there was no reason for people still to exist. But everyone else in the twenty-first century was so used to computers they didn't think a thing about it.

"Good morning," the computer said in a voice oozing empathy. Yep, the emotion sensor was still working. Unfortunately. "Would you care for information about adoption costs? Adoption laws? Adoption process and procedures? Adoption statistics? Availability of children to adopt? International adoptions?—"

Sometimes Melly really hated computers.

"No, no," she said irritably. "I don't need information that would help me adopt a child. I'm fifteen years old, for God's sake. I want to find someone to do the adopting."

The computer made a sound that could have passed for a gasp.

"Ah," it said. "Now I understand your anxiety. You are the victim of an unwanted pregnancy. And just a teenager . . . oh my. You need counseling, my dear. I don't mean to pressure you, and I certainly will not judge your actions, but you face several important choices. One should not rush too hastily into any of them. Shall I refer you to a counseling service right now?"

"No," Melly said. "Just show me a list of people wanting to adopt kids."

"But my dear—"

Melly switched off the computer's speakers. Seconds later the screen was flooded with images of happy families frolicking together in autumn leaves, playing pitch and catch, laughing together around a dinner table, building snowmen in a tree-lined yard. In spite of herself, Melly had to blink back tears.

She'd taken marketing classes once upon a time, she knew it was all just image. She lived near dozens of families and had never seen any of them act so happy together. But the videos got to her anyway.

Because she'd killed the voice option, the images were quickly replaced by text.

THE ADOPTION SITE! the screen trumpeted in large letters. Then, in smaller print, it urged, "Choose the family that's best for your baby!"

Then the screen filled with choices: race, creed, color, religion, spanking/no spanking, strong disciplinarians/lax disciplinarians, income level, professional standing, geographic preference, urban/suburban lifestyle, athletic/sedentary, intellectual/nonintellectual, casual/formal, pets/no pets, boaters, bikers, swimmers, aversion to water sports, cat people, dog people, ferret people . . .

Melly typed at the bottom, *"I don't care about any of that."*

"Congratulations! Your selection process resulted in" appeared on the screen. Melly waited. *"500,000 families!"* blinked out at her.

Melly gulped. She should have known. Birth control had been virtually perfected fifty years ago and made mandatory for all women from puberty onward, unless they and their mate could pass the rigorous Parent Test. So very few women had babies they didn't want. Meanwhile, medical ethicists had prevented cloning, and fertility problems had sky-rocketed because of environmental disasters. So there were lots of potential parents who wanted babies they couldn't have.

"Great," Melly muttered. "I'm going to be a hot commodity in about fifteen years."

"Would you like to see your selections?" the computer screen blinked at her. She hit *Y.* When the list of names scrolled out in front of her, she picked one at random.

"Sound, please," the computer prompted.

Sighing, Melly turned the speakers back on.

The screen showed a curtain opening.

"Have we got a family for you," boomed a male voice.

A couple stood on stage, waving.

"Hi! We're the Burnham-Toddy-Smythe-Wallaces!" the man said. "We have over seven million dollars in assets!"

"Oh, brother," Melly muttered. She zapped the Burnham-Toddy-Smythe-Wallaces and tried another choice. Two more beaming faces appeared on the screen.

"I'm Louis!"

"I'm Rachel!"

"We believe in the fellowship of humankind, and we believe it is our duty to raise a child to respect himself in the godhood of the world—"

Melly scrambled to get rid of Rachel and Louis as quickly as she could.

Sixty families later she was sitting with her face buried in her hands, the computer screen swimming with antique-style screen-saving fish, when Anny Beth strolled into the room.

"Hi," Anny Beth said. "Found Ozzie and Harriet yet?" It was a reference to an ancient TV show, one that had been on in their first lives. Neither of them could remember that, of course, but there had been reruns at the agency.

"Ozzie and Harriet died a hundred years ago," Melly moaned. "At this point I'd take Al and Peg Bundy over anyone in there." She pointed to the computer screen.

"*Married . . . with Children,*" Anny Beth said. "Cool. I thought I was the only one who watched that historical garbage. Can I be the wisecracking, dim-witted sexpot daughter?"

"Be my guest," Melly said. And then she burst into tears.

"Hey, hey," Anny Beth said. She patted Melly's shoulder. "It's okay. We'll find someone."

"I don't know if I'm crying for me"—Melly sniffed—"or the world. How can any of those people think they deserve a child?"

"They're desperate," Anny Beth said. "Desperate people always get weird. Don't forget that. And people who don't have kids yet have no clue what it's really like—remember?"

"I don't remember having children anymore," Melly said stiffly.

"Oh, right. I was the one who got pregnant at fifteen. Anyhow, are you convinced now that this is crazy? Why don't you come down and have lunch with me? I've got an hour before my next class. And don't you have to baby-sit this afternoon?"

Melly nodded. "But I'm not giving up. Maybe the answer is to find someone we already know, someone around here. The Rodneys are okay." They were the family she baby-sat for. They lived across the street.

"You'd trust them?" Anny Beth gave her a hard look.

Melly shrugged. "I don't know. If I got to know them better I might."

"You think the agency would let you tell them?"

"They couldn't really stop me, could they?" Melly asked.

Anny Beth grinned. "Now you sound like me!"

Melly blew her nose and reached to shut down the computer. Just then the computer announced, "You have mail!" and the screen-saving fish melted into an icon of a revolving letter.

"Stupid junk mail," Melly said. She clicked the letter open, then reached for the delete button. "All those stupid ads—"

"Wait!" Anny Beth had already read the message over Melly's shoulder.

Melly looked at the screen and instantly froze. The words glowed in terrifying green:

"Seeking information about Amelia Lenore Hazelwood, born Amelia Lenore Hibbard, April 21, 1900, in KY, possibly died December 15, 2000, in OH."

"Oh, no," Melly breathed.

MARGARET PETERSON HADDIX

March 26, 2001

One of the men saw it on TV first. Mr. Johnson started pounding on the nurse call button and the volume control button at the same time, and screaming out what everyone later figured out was, "One of us! One of us!"

The nurse arrived in time only to hear, "—the woman carried no identification. Police are searching missing persons reports. Anyone with information please call the number at the bottom of the screen." But, like Mr. Johnson, the nurse got a clear glimpse of the face on the screen: It was definitely Mrs. Swanson.

By the next news cycle a half an hour later everyone was assembled in the meeting room, staring at the four TVs the nurses had wheeled in. Amelia figured it was force of habit, because that was mostly what they did at the agency, have meetings. Certainly Dr. Reed and Dr. Jimson hadn't summoned anyone this time. They rushed in at the last minute, as one of the anchorwomen chuckled, "And we've got a strange story out of Bedford Hills tonight. . . ." A mug shot of Mrs. Swanson appeared above the anchor's head, and the attendants turned down the volume on the other three TVs.

"This woman appeared at the home of prominent attorney Morton Swanson this evening, claiming to be his mother, Louise Swanson. The real Mrs.

Swanson died several months ago. This woman created quite a disturbance. . . ."

The next view was video of Mrs. Swanson beating her fists on an imposing front door and screeching, "But I'm going to live forever, Morty! You never have to worry about losing me!" Then that scene was replaced by one of a reporter thrusting a microphone at a man in a tuxedo.

"You can only imagine the shock," the man said. "My mother was the dearest person on earth to me. And then to have that . . . that banshee claiming to be her . . ."

The reporter nodded sympathetically. "Did the impostor bear any resemblance to your, uh, deceased mother?"

The man frowned. "Well, she was old," he said doubtfully.

Amelia gasped, along with half the rest of the room. How could he not recognize his own mother?

On the TV the anchor appeared again, explaining that the woman claiming to be Mrs. Swanson had been taken into custody and was undergoing psychiatric evaluation, particularly in light of her claims of immortality.

Amelia watched Dr. Reed go ghostly pale. The TV station cut to a car commercial, and Dr. Jimson turned the volume down. Everyone sat in stunned silence until Mrs. Flick rolled her chair over to Dr. Reed.

"Why are you just standing there? Aren't you gonna go tell them people she ain't crazy?" she demanded.

"I-I-I don't know," he stammered.

"Well, she ain't, is she? If she's crazy, we all are," Mrs. Flick said, looking back at the rest of the crowd. Then people began to mutter, "Not me!" and "What's she mean?" But no one spoke loudly because they were all waiting for Dr. Reed's answer.

He sank into a chair beside the TVs and rubbed his temples.

"This is a problem I didn't anticipate," he said, almost as if speaking to himself. "I don't know what to do. If I save her, I betray the rest of you. It's protecting one person versus protecting forty-nine."

People began squirming in their chairs. Nobody seemed to understand.

Dr. Jimson stood watching Dr. Reed coldly from across the room.

"Fifty lives," she snapped. "We are responsible for fifty lives. You find a way to protect them all."

"I-I don't know," Dr. Reed repeated.

Amelia felt like a little kid watching her parents fight. Except her father had been the strong one, not her mother.

Dr. Jimson threw up her hands. "I have had it with you!" she exploded. "What is this—you do one nervy thing in your whole life, and then you're paralyzed with fear forever after? We did this!" She swung her arm in a broad sweep that indicated the entire crowd. "These are our people, like it or not. And we have to take care of them all!"

She spun on her heel. Afterward everyone would debate about whether she would have really done it, stormed into the office, picked up the phone, and called the number on the TV screen. But Dr. Reed stopped her with a single question.

"Why don't we ask them what they think?" He pointed at the crowd.

Dr. Jimson slowly turned around. But she didn't move any closer to Dr. Reed.

"Fine," she said. "Go ahead."

Her words fell into silence. Amelia waited for someone else to speak. Of course it was Mrs. Flick who rolled forward.

"Maybe it's just me," she started, "but I don't rightly understand what all the fuss's about. What's stopping you from just going and picking her up?"

"I'd have to explain," Dr. Reed said weakly.

Mrs. Flick shrugged. "Just say you run a funny farm and she escaped."

"I'd have to show ID," Dr. Reed said. "Credentials."

"Fake 'em," Mrs. Flick said. "How close they gonna look? They're probably dying to get rid of her."

But nobody was watching Mrs. Flick and Dr. Reed anymore. Mrs. Swanson's face had shown up on another TV screen, and now the anchor was clearly making an effort to look mournful. Dr. Jimson picked up a remote and turned off the mute button.

"—sad ending to the strange disturbance in a swank Bedford Hills neighborhood this afternoon. A woman claiming to be the mother of prominent attorney Morton Swanson stormed his home and had to be taken into custody. His real mother is dead—and now so, too, is the impostor." The crowd's collective gasp drowned out the anchor's next few words. Then Amelia heard, "—committed suicide—" before her ears seemed to stop working. Before, when she'd thought she was on the verge of death, she'd done that a lot, shut out the outside world without even trying. She'd been living mostly in her own mind, in her memories. But she wasn't on the verge of death anymore. If the doctors were right, she was on the verge of a new life, and she'd have to face whatever that meant. She opened her eyes—not having been conscious before that they were even shut—and looked around.

On TV the anchor had moved on to a new story, something about a fire in the bad section of the city. But no one was paying attention to the TV. Everyone looked as if a bomb had been dropped in their midst. Up at the front Dr. Reed had his face buried in his hands and was weeping. Amelia wasn't used to seeing men cry. It disturbed her. If he couldn't stop himself, she wanted someone else to lead him away, make him do it privately. After a long while Dr. Jimson went over to him, but all she did was lay her hands comfortingly on his shoulders. Dr. Reed began burbling, "I'm sorry. I'm so sorry. It's all my fault—"

"Don't say that," Dr. Jimson said. "You kept her alive longer than she would have lived otherwise—"

"But the way she died, by her own hand, feeling betrayed . . ."

Dr. Jimson nodded, as if agreeing on his guilt. Everyone sat in silence for a long time, listening to Dr. Reed cry. Then Mrs. Flick spoke up.

"Reckon it won't do Louise any good now," she said. "But seems like you've got some explaining to do to the rest of us."

Dr. Reed nodded but was too choked up to speak right away. Afterward, when Amelia asked Mrs. Flick how she'd known Dr. Reed was hiding something, she said, "Honey, I've seen a lot of guilty men in my day. And he was acting the guiltiest."

Dr. Reed blew his nose and began talking. "I lied," he confessed softly.

"Speak up!" someone yelled from the back.

"I lied," he repeated, his voice louder but not

stronger. "I lied to all of you, and I lied to Dr. Jimson and all our research assistants."

"So we're not going to live forever," someone grumbled. "Should have known."

"No"—Dr. Reed raised his head—"I didn't lie about that. It's true enough, as far as I know. It's just that I only gave PT-1 to one bunch of lab rats before I gave it to you. I didn't get FDA approval for this experiment. This is totally illegal."

"So?" Mrs. Flick asked.

Dr. Jimson bit her lip. "They don't understand," she told Dr. Reed. "They're not scientists." She turned back to the crowd. "There are certain, uh, protocols that must be followed for experiments on human subjects. Things to protect you. We have to be as sure as possible that an experiment is likely to be beneficial, not harmful. I won't go into all the details, but only testing a drug on a hundred lab animals before introducing it to humans is akin to"— she glanced at Dr. Reed with an unusual show of compassion—"plotting murder."

"Aw, don't be so hard on yourself, Doc." It was Mr. Johnson. Somehow the excitement had made him more articulate. "We was all going to die anyway."

Dr. Jimson shook her head. "That doesn't matter," she said. "Rules are rules. And in this case there were lots of ethical issues that needed to be worked out."

"But you signed on too." Amelia couldn't see how Dr. Jimson could be innocent if Dr. Reed was guilty. "Weren't you worried about those 'ethical issues'?"

"I gave her extensive fake documentation," Dr. Reed said without looking up. "I convinced her I had all my ducks in a row—"

"And I was eager to participate in the most momentous scientific experiment of my lifetime," Dr. Jimson admitted. "I'm guilty too."

"We hadn't figured out what your lives would be like as you unaged. We didn't think about the need to keep secrets from your families. We didn't think about what could or couldn't be revealed to the media," Dr. Reed said.

"I don't get it," Mrs. Flick said. From all the puzzled expressions in the room, Amelia thought Mrs. Flick spoke for everyone. "You didn't know any of us from Adam. Right? It didn't matter to you if we lived or died. Why was you in such a dad-blamed hurry?"

"My grandmother—" Dr. Reed choked up again. "My grandmother was dying. She was very dear to me—I couldn't not try to save her. . . ."

Everyone looked around, as if wondering why Dr. Reed's grandmother hadn't claimed kinship before. Dr. Reed answered the unspoken question.

"She died anyway," he said softly. "There were

originally one hundred of you. But no one pulled through who had had certain types of health problems—a history of stroke, heart disease, and diabetes, among other things."

It was hard not to get sucked in by the grief in his voice. But there was too much else to figure out to take time feeling sorry. Amelia looked around, wondering if everyone was as confused as she was. Her brain hadn't had such a workout in years, if ever. Only Mrs. Flick looked up to ask another question.

"I'm sorry about your grammy and all," she said, "but I still don't get it. Maybe you'll have to talk a little slower. I only went up to fifth grade before I had to drop out, so this science stuff is kind of too much for me. Why didn't you just sneak into your grandmother's room in the dark of night and inject some of that PT-1 in her butt? Why mess with the rest of us and all your lies?"

"I needed Dr. Jimson," Dr. Reed admitted. "I won't go into all the technicalities, but I didn't trust myself to figure out how to translate PT-1 to human conditions. She's more experienced than I. And I knew she was too ethical to sign on to an experiment just for emotional reasons. So . . . I needed the rest of you to get her."

"I didn't know Dr. Reed's grandmother was one of the subjects," Dr. Jimson said self-righteously. "That was unethical too."

The room was silent again, except for the TVs babbling. Then Mrs. Flick rolled over and turned all of them off. She waited until all eyes were on her.

"Okay," she said. "I've had enough of this belly-aching and hand-wringing. Dr. Reed, Dr. Jimson, you got to quit letting that guilt eat you up. What's done's done. So some people died. So what? Their number was up. So that weasel Morty Swanson got a little shaken up. I'd say he deserved it for never visiting his mother in the nursing home. Didn't even recognize her . . . So Louise didn't exactly die a Christian death—I'd say that's between her and God, and we can't worry about it. I say it's time we get grateful for what these doctors did, whether they feel good about it or not. They worked a miracle. I'm here to tell you I messed up my first life right bad, and I'm tickled pink to get another chance. I plan to enjoy it."

In the back someone started clapping. The applause spread. Dr. Reed and Dr. Jimson looked around in astonishment. Dr. Jimson even blushed.

"But what about Louise? And our families—," someone half whined. It was Mrs. Rivers, who'd spent a lot of time with Mrs. Swanson.

"Louise made her choice, and we've got to make ours. I say we agree none of the rest of us are going to contact our families. I'll tell you why. We tell our kids, and our kids' kids, and maybe their kids, and that's too many people knowing. They'll want some of this PT stuff too, and the docs ain't handing it out to all comers, right?" Behind Mrs. Flick, Dr. Jimson shook her head in an emphatic no. Dr. Reed joined in a second later, looking regretful. Mrs. Flick went on. "If you worried about your kids fighting over who got Aunt Mary's good china, and who got Uncle George's gun collection, think about what this battle'd be like! Who's with me on this?"

Amelia thought about saying, "Wait a minute. You don't even like your family. What right do you have to tell the rest of us to give up the people we love most?" But for that moment, at least, she could see Mrs. Flick's point. She thought back decades to the time one of her boys, Burrell, had got his hand caught in a corn picker the autumn he was twelve. The hand got infected, and the doctor who rode out to look at it said he'd have to cut it off; otherwise, the infection would spread and Burrell might die. Amelia thought she wouldn't be able to bear it, but she heard Roy say, "Then do it." And after that Amelia never looked back, never wondered if the hand might have healed, if it should have been saved. She cleaned and bandaged Burrell's stump every day for weeks, answering every one of his complaints, "Well, it had to be done. God let you live, so you've got to live the best you can." This was the same kind of decision, requiring a clean cut, no regrets.

"I'm with you," she announced.

Around her others began to mumble agreement too. At last only Mrs. Rivers hadn't spoken. Everyone looked her way.

"Oh, all right," she grumbled. "I'm with you too."

A cheer went up, and Dr. Reed went around thanking everyone and shaking hands. Later Amelia would remember the next hour in the meeting room as one of the happiest in her entire life—her second life. People hugged one another. Dr. Reed and Dr. Jimson started kissing, right in front of their patients. Everyone danced, with or without wheelchairs. Nobody cared. Someone brought out champagne, and they all toasted Dr. Jimson and Dr. Reed and one another. A few people also toasted the memory of Louise Swanson. That reminded Dr. Reed to toast his grandmother as well, "whose death led to the second lives of all these people." Amelia thought that was simplifying things too much, but she didn't say so. She wasn't used to champagne. The bubbles tickled her nose. As everyone around her pledged eternal loyalty to Dr. Reed and Dr. Jimson and the agency and one another, Amelia leaned over and whispered to Mrs. Flick, "I thought you said this thing was a curse."

Mrs. Flick shrugged. "Maybe I changed my mind."

"Only 'maybe'?" Amelia asked. "You're not sure?"

But Mrs. Flick was swept away onto the dance floor before she could answer.

April 22, 2085

Melly tried to fight the rising tide of panic as she stared at the glowing E-mail. Someone wanted to find her. Someone doubted the official records saying she had died. Soon her name and likeness would be splashed on computer screens across the world as a freak. She wouldn't have to look for parents—all those 500,000 weirdos would come after her, beseeching her to be their child.

"Oh, no," she repeated. "Oh, no." She felt too dizzy to think clearly.

"Will you just chill out?" Anny Beth muttered. "This may be totally innocent. . . ."

In a daze, Melly watched Anny Beth punching buttons on the computer.

"Recent newscasts," Anny Beth muttered. "Something connected to genealogy."

In seconds Anny Beth had some TV show up on the computer screen. A blow-dried anchor type was confidently asserting, "People of all walks of life are trying to find out whose footsteps they're walking in, so to speak—"

"Why is it," Anny Beth asked, "that with everything else that's improved in the last eighty years, TV news still stinks?"

Melly didn't answer. The anchor was talking about how interest in genealogy was overwhelming once again, surpassing even the *Roots* craze of the late 1900s.

"The information about your family history is out there," he said solemnly. "You just have to find it."

The shot cut to a gray-bearded expert who began describing a popular method of searching: "It's called saturation. You just tell your computer to E-mail everyone in the world with the same last name as you."

Anny Beth zapped the TV broadcast off the screen, and the E-mail reappeared. It didn't look quite so threatening anymore, especially when Anny Beth asked the computer, "Sender?" and the computer replied, "A. J. Hazelwood. Do you need to know more?"

"Nope," Anny Beth said.

"How did you know?" Melly asked.

Anny Beth shrugged. "I watch a lot more TV than you do. And you know my memory—steel trap. At least for this lifetime." She slapped her hands together. Melly wondered if there were a single other person alive who could watch that motion and bring up a mental picture of metal teeth clamping down on a raccoon's leg. More and more she felt like she was living in a foreign land, because her most vivid memories were of a different time and place. Oh, well, she'd forget hunting and trapping soon enough.

"Want to get rid of it?" Anny Beth asked, her finger hovering over the delete button for the E-mail.

"Shouldn't we tell the agency?"

"And have them bring out the E.T. SWAT team? I don't think so." Decades ago, not long after they left the agency, Anny Beth had fallen in love with the movie *E.T.* She'd watched it over and over, until one day she quit, cold turkey. She confessed the reason only to Melly: that she'd begun having nightmares that she was on her own, living a normal life, when suddenly scientists in space suits swarmed her home and hooked her up to monitors, just like E.T. Only in her nightmare the scientists were followed by TV journalists thrusting microphones in her face. Anny Beth and Melly had done their best to turn their fears into jokes. They didn't think the agency would ever whisk them away against their will, but they could never laugh wholeheartedly at each other's "E.T. SWAT team" jokes.

"All right," Melly said. "But leave the message. I still want to think about it."

"Don't answer it," Anny Beth warned.

"Do you think I'm crazy?" Melly asked. But she couldn't explain to Anny Beth why she wanted to hold on to the message. Just a few more hours, just a day— now that she wasn't frightened by it, the message made her feel good. She liked the thought that someone she was related to wanted to remember who she'd been.

"See, what'll happen is, one of your descendants will write back to this A. J. person and tell her all about being dragged to her great-grandmother's funeral when she was only six or seven, and about how scary you looked in that coffin—"

"I wasn't in any coffin," Melly said sharply. "Remember, all our families agreed to donate our bodies to science? They knew they weren't burying us."

"Yeah, but they never said whether they had us posed at the funeral beforehand. And think about it—in Kentucky? Back then? Got to have an open casket."

Melly knew Anny Beth was just teasing, but it still disturbed her. From the beginning the agency had discouraged curiosity about how the fake funerals had been conducted, how the families had handled the details. Once everyone had agreed not to contact their children or grandchildren or great-grandchildren, Dr. Reed and Dr. Jimson wanted all their patients to forget their families entirely. They even brought in a psychologist to counsel them. The psychologist was told only that she was dealing with a bunch of elderly people who were irreversibly estranged from their offspring. Melly had hated that meeting. She would have sobbed if she'd been that kind of a person.

Now Anny Beth was warming up to an imitation of Melly's supposed great-grandchild. "And my mamaw took me up to the casket and made me look in, and I tell you, I was so scared I thought I'd pee my pants. Then I saw this face that was like wax, except someone put too much makeup on it. Then I started giggling so hard I did pee my pants, and my mamaw tanned my hide, right there, for disrespecting the dead—"

Melly couldn't help laughing.

"I think you've got my funeral mixed up with your own," she taunted. "But you do a great old-lady imitation."

Anny Beth backed away from the computer desk to give a fake bow.

"Imitations are my specialty," she said, rising from the bow with a graceful flourish. "You should see my teenager impression." A sad look crossed her face. "Do you ever get confused about what's an imitation and what's real?"

"It's all the same," Melly said, shutting her computer down.

They went down to lunch and clowned around until it was time for Anny Beth to leave for class and Melly to go baby-sit for the Rodneys. Kicking her shoes against the foam-rubber pavement as she walked across the street, Melly thought back to the E-mailed genealogy request. It was a shame, really, that she couldn't write back to this A. J. Hazelwood and tell him or her everything about growing up in rural Kentucky. She could tell her grandfather's stories about fighting in the Civil War, her grandmother's stories about helping fugitive slaves go north. . . . What genealogist wouldn't kill for something like that?

Her mind still on the past, Melly knocked on the Rodneys' door. Then she remembered what century she was in and punched the automated video-screen doorbell.

"Melly the baby-sitter is here," a disembodied voice announced, the doorbell having recognized her fingerprint instantly.

"Oh, Melly, come on in," Mrs. Rodney's voice floated out of an unseen speaker.

The door opened on its own, and Melly stepped over the threshold into the foyer. The sounds of a computer game came from the next room. It was Melly's opinion that kids in this century spent entirely too much time glued to their computers, but nobody had asked her. Mrs. Rodney came down the stairs, her beehive hairdo towering as high as ever. It swayed slightly as she walked.

"Melly, little Logan Junior has come down with a bad cold, so we won't be needing you today. But I wanted to talk to you about something." Mrs. Rodney peered intently into Melly's face. Melly felt like she was being given a test—one Mrs. Rodney had already decided she would fail.

"And what is that?" Melly asked, as politely as possible.

"How old are you? Honestly?"

Melly hesitated. It had been so much easier even a few years ago, when she was in her twenties. People never expected grown-ups to be truthful about their age. She'd been able to live in the same place for entire decades without anyone noticing anything suspicious. Now that her unaging was going to be more conspicuous, would she have to start moving every year? How would she ever find someone to take care of her then?

"You have to answer, my dear," Mrs. Rodney said. "As the employer of an age-challenged individual—"

Melly stifled the instinct to giggle. Oh, if Mrs. Rodney knew what a challenge Melly's real age was!

"I have every right to ask for that information," Mrs. Rodney finished. "And I have the right to check your records if I want."

Melly gave up. She knew Mrs. Rodney was right.

"I'm fifteen," she muttered. That's what her records would say now. The agency changed them every year.

Mrs. Rodney leaned away from Melly, so far back that Melly half feared her beehive would topple her.

"That's interesting," Mrs. Rodney said. "I'm sure you said you were sixteen when we first hired you a year and a half ago."

"Maybe I said, 'almost sixteen,'" Melly mumbled.

Mrs. Rodney tapped her foot. "Hmm. If you were almost sixteen a year and a half ago, wouldn't that make you sixteen now? Or—more likely, seventeen?" Melly had heard Mrs. Rodney use exactly this tone with Logan Junior, who was barely five. Melly felt the same kind of powerless rage a child feels. She suddenly sympathized with Logan Junior for his many out-of-control tantrums. But she was much too old for tantrums.

"Have you had any complaints about my work?" Melly asked stiffly.

"No," Mrs. Rodney replied. "Not until now. But this makes me wonder—if you lied to me about your age, what else would you lie about? Anyhow, I really want a baby-sitter who could drive Logan Junior to the hospital in an emergency. I thought you said you could do that."

"I . . ." Melly knew she had no defense. Why hadn't she anticipated this conversation? Had she been risking exposing her secret by baby-sitting at all? And how could she have ever possibly thought Mrs. Rodney might be the person she wanted as a surrogate mother in the coming years?

"I'm sorry, dear," Mrs. Rodney said, settling back into sweetness now that she'd made her point. "I'm sure you'll understand this when you're a bit more mature. Here's some money to thank you for your time today."

She shoved a folded bill into Melly's pocket. Then, before Melly fully realized it, Mrs. Rodney had spun her around and propelled her toward the door.

"Good-bye, dear," Mrs. Rodney said. "I hope there are no hard feelings. Logan Junior thinks very highly of you. I'm sure we'll see you around the neighborhood."

Melly couldn't answer. She stomped out the door and back into her own house. How dare Mrs. Rodney act like that! Even if Melly only counted her second lifetime, Melly had been taking care of kids since before Mrs. Rodney was out of diapers. Melly even had a master's degree in early childhood education, not that her alma mater would recognize her anymore. It just wasn't fair that Melly couldn't defend herself with all the facts.

Back in her own bedroom Melly flung herself across the bed and sobbed into her pillow. Being a teenager stunk. Why hadn't she remembered how bad it was—mostly having to act like a grown-up but still being treated like a child? And it was worse now because she really was a grown-up, no matter how young she looked and felt. She raised her head and stared into the mirror above the bureau.

Her brown hair hung long and straight on either side of her face, in the style of the day. Her features were delicate—the last time she'd been fifteen, she'd been proud of her rosebud mouth but despaired of her button nose. Of course, nobody nowadays compared features to anything as rustic as flowers or buttons. What were they now—light-switch-size nose, computer-icon-shaped mouth? The thought made her grin, in spite of herself, revealing the small chip in her front tooth. It was the remnant of a wild horse-and-buggy ride back in 1912. The agency people always marveled at her teeth—she was the only one in Project Turnabout who still had her original set. (Of course, even her teeth wouldn't have survived if it hadn't been for the invention of Perfect Toothpaste in the early 2030s.) The last dentist she'd gone to, back in 2025, before the occupation went the way of blacksmiths and typewriter manufacturers, had wanted to fix the chipped tooth. "It would be such an easy thing," he had wheedled. But Melly had refused, without explaining why. That chip had been with her for more than a century. It was one of the things she counted on about herself, one of the things that didn't change with age. She didn't cheat at cards, she liked licorice, she had a chipped front tooth. "She didn't lie" would have been on the list once too, but Project Turnabout had changed all that.

Now she switched on the bureau lamp, hoping the brighter light would scare up some wrinkles, make her look older. But, no—her skin was as smooth and taut as any teenager's. Between the long hair, the small face, and the chipped tooth, she could pass for much younger than fifteen—maybe even twelve. No wonder Mrs. Rodney was suspicious.

Melly was just beginning to feel some forgiveness for the other woman when the phone rang. Melly quickly wiped her eyes and nose, and switched on the receiver port on her computer. Mrs. Rodney's face appeared on the screen.

"Oh, Melly, I'm such a ninny. I forgot to tell you—before I asked you about your age—someone called my house yesterday. A woman named A. J. Hazelwood."

Melly felt her brow begin to furrow, her jaw begin to drop in astonishment. She could believe that someone might be E-mailing every Hazelwood on the planet. But calling? And calling neighbors? This was serious. Someone was definitely after her. *Don't think about it. Act normal for Mrs. Rodney,* she told herself. *Get rid of her and then worry.*

Fortunately Mrs. Rodney was still talking. "She just left a message on my machine because I was in the bathtub at the time. . . . She said she was trying to get in touch with you, but you and your sister have unlisted numbers, so she was calling neighbors—you aren't in any trouble, are you?"

"No, no, of course not," Melly replied, struggling to keep her voice even, her expression bland. Why in the world had people thought it was a good thing to see each other on the telephone?

"Well, I just wondered because—I know I'm probably out of line asking this, but you know I'm just concerned for you—you and your sister aren't runaways, are you?"

Melly forced out a laugh, trying to make it sound surprised and insulted and childish all at once. "Is that what you thought? Oh, no. Believe me, Anny Beth and I aren't runaways."

But suddenly she understood. Mrs. Rodney hadn't really been worried about Melly being too young to take care of Logan Junior at all. She was afraid that Melly was a runaway. Melly vaguely remembered hearing something in the news about people being arrested for taking advantage of runaway children.

"So who is this A. J. Hazelwood?" Mrs. Rodney asked.

Melly scrunched up her face, as if she was thinking hard. Which she was.

"I think I remember something about some old relative—a great-aunt or somebody—with those initials," Melly said. "I'll ask Anny Beth."

Melly could tell Mrs. Rodney wasn't entirely convinced.

"Why didn't this A. J. person ask for Anny Beth instead of you? Since she's older."

"Maybe it's because of the name. You know, since Anny Beth's the first child, she has my dad's name, Flick, and since I'm second, I have my mom's name, Hazelwood." For perhaps the first time in her second lifetime Melly was glad that society was really confused about what to do with inherited names. "It's probably nothing. Can I have the woman's number?"

"Maybe I should call her for you. . . ."

It took every bit of acting skill Melly had learned in the past eighty-four years to pretend that that suggestion didn't worry her. "I guess you could, but I'm sure Anny Beth will want to talk to her too. Then that would be two calls. And aren't the authorities discouraging unnecessary calls? To keep the phone lines free for standard computer use or something?"

Mrs. Rodney flushed on the computer screen, and Melly realized she'd scored a direct hit. The authorities would probably consider Mrs. Rodney's call to Melly unnecessary, since they lived so close.

"So what's the number?" Melly forged on.

Mumbling, Mrs. Rodney told her.

"But you'll let me know what this is about?" Mrs. Rodney added.

"Sure," Melly said, thinking, *Not on your life.*

"Well, then," Mrs. Rodney said. "If this all clears

up, maybe you can come over and we can talk some more about whether you're responsible enough to take care of Logan Junior. Maybe with some supervision . . ."

Melly decided Logan Junior must really be driving her crazy this afternoon and she hadn't been able to find another baby-sitter. But Melly didn't have time to worry about Mrs. Rodney's problems.

"Hmm," she said noncommittally. "Hey, I think I hear Anny Beth calling. Gotta go. See you later, Mrs. R."

Melly shut down the connection. Once she didn't have to act for Mrs. Rodney, her hands began shaking too hard for her to type on the computer. She switched on the verbal command system.

"Computer," she directed. "Get that E-mail message I received yesterday and tell me everything in the sender's data profile."

"Yes, ma'am," the computer said.

In the second it took the computer to search for what Melly wanted, Melly heard Anny Beth come in downstairs. *Got to tell her,* Melly thought disjointedly. *Got to find out—*

The computer began answering.

"Sender has blocked all information except name and occupation," the computer said.

"And they are?" Melly asked. She was trembling violently now.

"A. J. Hazelwood. Reporter," the computer said.

Melly scrambled up so quickly her chair flipped backward.

"Anny Beth!" she screamed. "Start packing. We've got to get out of here!"

PART TWO

April 23, 2085

We're in a hotel now, after driving all night. Anny Beth thinks we're safe.

"But you used your debit card to pay the bill. And can't our license be traced by satellite?" I protested.

"Didn't you pay any attention in privacy class in college?" she asked. "All that stuff's off-limits. Except for cops. And as far as I know, we don't have the police after us."

Still. I don't trust reporters.

I made Anny Beth plug in her computer so we could see the TV news. Earthquakes in Mexico, typhoons in India, some political scandal out of Washington. Nothing about two super-old ladies who happen to look like teenagers. So maybe Anny Beth's right, and we are safe. But how did this reporter find out about me in the first place? And why does she have my name?

Anny Beth's still watching TV. A game show. The category's twentieth-century history. I don't think she's got a single question right yet, which is pretty funny when you think about it. She just threw a pillow at the computer screen.

I feel like throwing things too. But I'm not that kind of a person. Am I? I don't really feel like I know who I am. It's something about being in a hotel room—I think they're the same the world over now. Same sterile glasses by the ice bucket. Same stainless-steel countertops in the bathroom. Same bland white disposable bedding. It all says, "Who are you to have an identity when I don't?"

I've had so many identities in my lifetime I hardly remember them all. The first time around I was always pretty much the same person. I just got older. But this time . . . I even changed my name. The first thirty years or so I was Amelia, the old lady. Then I was Amy for years and years. That was when I was a nurse, when I was a preschool teacher, when I was busy, busy, busy. I didn't become Melly until I turned twenty and people started reacting to "Amy" with wrinkled noses and comments like, "What—were you named after your great-grandmother? Yuck!" I guess "Amy" was so associated with the 1960s and 1970s that no one could believe a young girl would be called that.

You wouldn't think it would matter, but I felt different when I was Amelia, when I was Amy, when I became Melly. I envy Anny Beth, who has always been just herself. She's the same here as she would be at home or on Mars.

I don't know why I'm babbling on about names and identities when I should be focused on practical matters. Finding a new place to live. Getting new E-mail identities. Starting new lives. We'll have to

MARGARET PETERSON HADDIX

notify the agency, of course, but Anny Beth and I agreed we should sleep on it first so we'll have the strength to resist their suggestions. We already know what they'll say: "Come back. Come back."

When we were in the car, driving and driving and driving, we each made a list of what really mattered to us. (It's some exercise Anny Beth learned about at college.) "Not getting caught by that reporter" was only number two.

Number one on both of our lists was still "Staying out of the agency."

Dr. Reed and Dr. Jimson got married.

They had one ceremony for all their friends and family "on the outside," then a second in the conference room at the agency. Cheers went up when the justice of the peace declared them "man and wife."

Afterward, while Amelia waited in line for punch, she heard the justice of the peace congratulating Dr. Reed again before leaving. She had a new hearing aid in that amplified different sounds. Her last hearing aid dated back to the 1980s, when she first began going deaf; it hadn't seemed worth updating when she was about to die. But now the agency was urging all sorts of new things on them. She was still adjusting to being able to hear people talk several yards away. So she listened intently to Dr. Reed and the justice.

"I must say," the justice of the peace said in his clipped, educated-sounding voice, "I've never seen a group of nursing home residents so devoted to their director."

"Oh, they're just like our children, to Trina and me," Dr. Reed said.

Amelia turned enough to see the justice's puzzled expression.

"Don't you mean grandparents?" he asked.

Dr. Reed laughed. "Oh, some old people have a

lot in common with kids," he said, and exuberantly shook the justice's hand again.

The nurse's aide handed Amelia her punch then, warning, "There's a lot of sherbet in that one. Very rich!" and Amelia lost track of the other conversation. She rolled her chair forward and automatically put the cup to her lips, but the treat was tainted for her now. Did Dr. Reed and Dr. Jimson really consider Amelia and the others mere children? Kids? She longed to go over and tell him off, but it seemed a little rude at his own wedding. She could wait. She had years and years and years now.

"Hey, Mrs. Hazelwood! Come on over here!" It was Dr. Jimson beckoning her toward the cake table.

After Dr. Reed's comments Dr. Jimson's tone seemed a little too familiar, but Amelia decided she was being overly sensitive. She steered her chair toward Dr. Jimson. Dr. Jimson bent down and put her arms around Amelia's shoulders.

"Happy birthday!" she said.

Amelia gaped. Was it really her birthday? What was the date? Back at the nursing home they'd had calendars everywhere, as if to make the residents think they'd made some great accomplishment just by surviving another day. But here the calendars were in the background. A day, even a year, no longer had the same significance.

But evidently birthdays were still noteworthy.

Dr. Reed tapped a fork against a glass to get everyone's attention. People began gathering around the doctors and the cake table.

"Speech! Speech!" someone yelled. It was Mr. Johnson. Ever since the night Louise died, he had become increasingly talkative.

Dr. Reed laughed appreciatively. Dr. Jimson unwrapped her arms from around Amelia and stepped forward. "We just wanted to share this happy occasion—"

"No, no, let the man do the talking!" Mr. Johnson hollered.

Dr. Jimson looked at Dr. Reed and shrugged. Dr. Reed cleared his throat.

"This is a wonderful day for Trina and me," he said. "But it's also a momentous time for someone in the project: We are now able to celebrate the first birthday since you all came out of your comas. Amelia Hazelwood, would you mind . . . ?"

He pushed Amelia's chair around behind the cake table. Beside the three-story wedding cake someone had placed a large sheet cake. Amelia squinted, trying to read the upside-down words spelled out in pastel pink frosting: HAPPY 1-0—

"Can you blow out the candle?" Dr. Reed urged before she'd had time to scan the whole phrase. She might be unaging, but she still thought young people hurried things too much. She puffed in the general direction of the cake and got lucky. The candle flame flickered and went out. Without the glare from the candle on her cataracts, she could read the whole cake: HAPPY 100TH BIRTHDAY, AMELIA!

"Shouldn't that be—," she started to protest, but Dr. Reed was in the midst of urging everyone to sing "Happy Birthday." They finally ended, "Happy birthday to you!" with Dr. Reed's booming bass voice drowning out all the scratchy old voices and Dr. Jimson's monotone alto. Everyone watched Amelia expectantly. She was supposed to say something nice, to thank the doctors for allowing her to reach this milestone.

"I already turned one hundred before," she said. "On my last birthday. I'm one hundred and one now."

Dr. Reed laughed merrily. "Yes and no. You were born one hundred and one years ago, true, but you have not aged another year since you turned one hundred. Rather, you've reversed the process. So my wife and I"—he paused to flash a loving glance at Dr. Jimson—"we decided it would be most useful to start counting back with each birthday our patients have. This is your hundredth birthday but it marks the end of being one hundred, not the beginning. You are ninety-nine now. And next year you will have your ninety-ninth birthday and become ninety-eight."

Once upon a time, years and years ago when she was a schoolgirl, Amelia had been good at math. So she understood what he meant. But it still made no sense. It bothered her. She liked counting forward. She wanted credit for the years she'd lived. This way, she felt like she'd lost something.

"Does it have to be that way?" she asked, sounding sulkier than she meant to.

Dr. Reed laughed again, but not nearly so merrily. "No. We're breaking new ground. We're setting the rules ourselves." He exchanged a glance with Dr. Jimson that seemed to exclude everyone else in the room—as if by "we" he only meant him and her. Amelia told herself she was still upset about the conversation she'd overheard; all newlyweds exchanged exclusionary glances like that. Dr. Reed went on. "You can count your age any way you want. You can use binary numbers, for all I care. But when you're walking around with the body of a twenty-five-year-old, it won't be very meaningful to call yourself one hundred seventy-five."

Amelia frowned, thinking.

"So if you freeze our ages at, say, twenty-five," she said slowly, "we'll turn twenty-five every year."

"Something like that," Dr. Reed said with a grin. He gave Amelia a hearty pat on the back. "You'll be like those birthday cards that joke about every birthday being the twenty-ninth. Except it won't be a joke for you. You really won't age!"

Amelia's frown deepened. She had never lied

about her age, never fought the advances of gray hair or crow's-feet or the march of time. She thought birthdays meant something: an additional year of life and, hopefully, wisdom gained. Yes, she'd regretted the losses that had come with age: the loss of sight and hearing and taste and smell, the loss of mobility, the loss of people she loved. But she'd still counted each year as a gain. Unaging should make each year even more of a gain. Why was she so hung up on a mere number?

People were waiting for her to say something, to announce her joy at being only ninety-nine again. But she wasn't one to think out loud, and she still had to think this through. The waiting silence began to weigh on her.

Then, "Ain't nobody going to cut that cake?" a voice called out. It was Mrs. Flick. Amelia shot her a grateful smile.

Later Mrs. Flick rolled her wheelchair up to the table beside Amelia while she ate her cake. Mrs. Flick put her own cake plate beside Amelia's and dug in. She chewed and swallowed, then looked over at Amelia.

"We sure got a lot to think on around here, don't we?" Mrs. Flick asked.

Amelia nodded silently.

Mrs. Flick gazed out at the center of the room, which had been cleared of chairs and turned into a dance floor. Amelia followed her friend's gaze. Dr. Jimson and Dr. Reed were dancing together, their arms wrapped around each other's waist. A few of the nurses and aides had led some of the patients out onto the dance floor as well, making mismatched couples. An aide who looked to be barely out of her teens bent down to hold Mr. Johnson's hands as he swayed in his wheelchair. Another patient was trying to teach a nurse to do the Charleston. Big-band-era music swelled around all of them. Amelia wondered if the music was the doctors' choice, or if it was what they assumed their patients would like.

"So," Mrs. Flick said. "Was it like this the last time you turned a hundred?"

"It—," Amelia started to answer, then something strange happened. She'd been thinking of her last birthday only a few moments ago, she knew, but suddenly the memory was like a fish that swam away just as she reached down to catch it. "I—," she started again, but the memory was gone, disappeared without a trace. "I don't know," she said uncertainly.

Amelia saw Dr. Reed mouth the word to Dr. Jimson: "Alzheimer's?" And she saw Dr. Jimson shake her head, ever so slightly. The puzzled frown deepened on Dr. Jimson's face.

"What's the last thing you remember?" Dr. Jimson asked gently.

"Seeing your husband whisper to you about whether or not I have Alzheimer's," Amelia replied tartly.

Dr. Jimson had the grace to look chagrined. She exchanged a look with Dr. Reed.

"No," she said. "I mean the last thing you remember before you took PT-1 and came to the agency."

Amelia thought back, honestly trying. This memory loss upset her more than she wanted to let on. That's why she had bothered to tell the doctors. It was the morning after her birthday now—she was ninety-nine again, she reminded herself—and she was absolutely certain she no longer remembered her first one hundredth birthday. Even the ghost of memory she'd thought she had, had slipped away.

"What do you remember about the year 2000?" Dr. Jimson prompted.

"There was a war in Africa," Amelia said.

"You remember that?" Dr. Jimson asked, a bit too

eagerly. Both she and Dr. Reed leaned forward expectantly.

"No," Amelia said. "I read about it in the newspaper this morning. There was a time line in the story about the peace talks."

Dr. Jimson gave a disappointed glance to the paper stacked neatly on Amelia's bedside table. "I mean, what do you remember that you knew then? What happened in your life? Where were you living?"

"Well, I know I was at the Riverside Nursing Home then, because I moved in in 1995—"

"Do you remember being there in 2000?"

Amelia frowned. How had 2000 been any different from 1999 or 1998? Riverside had been so dull. Not like the agency, where there were always tests and studies and questions and curious researchers to occupy her time. And improvements. Just last week she'd regained the ability to swing her legs over the side of the bed. And today she'd done her own hair.

At Riverside she'd only been waiting to die.

"I think, at Easter that year, I went to my son's family. George's. And maybe that was the last time I left the nursing home," Amelia said. She remembered because she'd heard one of her great-grandsons giggling at the dinner table, "Great-granny wears diapers just like a baby!" His parents had shushed him quickly, and Amelia pretended not to hear. She felt like saying, "Hey, I doubt if your bladder would do any better after eight pregnancies and a hundred years!" But then she looked around at the worried faces of her descendants and their spouses and suddenly wondered if that was all she had become: a worry. Just another mouth to feed, just another diaper to change, just as dependent and needy as a baby, without the chance of ever contributing anything again. Why had God kept her alive so long if she was so worthless?

"Someone can take me back now," she'd mumbled, though she'd only half finished her dessert. "I'm tired."

Now she turned to Dr. Jimson and assured her earnestly, "I do remember that Easter."

"Good," Dr. Jimson said. "But according to the nursing home records, that was Easter 1999, not 2000, that you went to your son's. Do you remember anything after that?"

"I don't know," Amelia said, suddenly irritated. "If you already know what happened from my records, why are you bothering to ask?"

"Because we're working on a hypothesis about your memory and Project Turnabout," Dr. Jimson said with more gentleness than Amelia would have expected. It made Amelia think the hypothesis was something bad. "We need to ask the others some questions too. Can you think of anything else we should know about what you do or don't remember?"

"No," Amelia mumbled, and lay back against her pillow.

But after the doctors were gone, she couldn't stop thinking about what she'd forgotten. She swung her legs over the side of the bed and back again, practicing while she thought. It made no sense. Her leg muscles were stronger, her hearing was better, even her appetite had improved. If everything else had got better with unaging, shouldn't her brain be improving too?

She swung her legs back and forth once more, thinking hard. She did feel like her brain had improved. She was sharper. She got more answers right on the crossword puzzle in the morning paper. Why should she be losing her memory about her own life? It was like a whole year had been erased when she hit her one hundredth birthday again.

A whole year.

Amelia turned with unaccustomed agility and slapped the nurse call button.

"Yes?" the nurse answered lazily over the intercom.

"Could Dr. Reed and Dr. Jimson come back, please?" Amelia said.

By the time the doctors returned, the full horror

of what Amelia was thinking had hit her. She was sitting with her head bowed, eyes closed in despair.

"Mrs. Hazelwood?" Dr. Jimson said gently.

Amelia didn't raise her head.

"When I turned one hundred again," she began slowly, "I think I lost all my memories of the first time I was one hundred."

Nobody said anything, so she went on.

"I remember everything since I came to the agency. I remember things from before I turned one hundred. But that one year of my life is gone. Are my memories being replaced? Is it that the longer I live, the more memories I'll lose?"

Her voice trembled. Amelia looked up in time to see the doctors exchange a glance. She could tell: They knew she was right.

"You can fix it, can't you?" Amelia asked.

Neither of the doctors answered her.

"That's what I was afraid of," Dr. Jimson said quietly, speaking to her husband, not Amelia.

Dr. Reed slammed his hand against the doorway.

"No! That can't be right. The brain can't work that way. There are thousands of unused neurons to store new memories in—why would new memories replace existing ones?"

"Because the brain is unaging too, following the same patterns it followed the first time around," Dr. Jimson said. "It's like we hit the rewind and record buttons at the same time. So she's recording over her old memories."

"Not if she forgot an entire year in one day," Dr. Reed jeered.

"She didn't. I bet she's been forgetting all along—all of them have. Remember how we thought they all had temporary amnesia about signing the waiver forms? But nobody missed any other old memories until her birthday came along. That was the first significant memory anyone lost," Dr. Jimson said.

It made sense to Amelia, even though she didn't want it to.

"You can fix it, can't you?" she asked again. "I don't want to forget everything."

Out of habit it was Dr. Reed she appealed to, not Dr. Jimson. He was the one who'd played God and begun her unaging. He was the one who was going to make her young again and keep her that way. Surely he knew how to fix a little thing like memory.

But it was Dr. Jimson who answered first.

"Honestly, I don't know what we can do," she said. "I'm sorry. There's still so much humans don't understand about the brain. But we'll do the best we can."

Dr. Reed glared at his wife.

"Don't say it like that," he said. He came to Amelia's bedside and patted her hand. "I promise you, Mrs. Hazelwood, we'll find a way to fix this problem. And maybe we can find a way to restore your memories. Maybe they're not really gone, just . . . inaccessible."

Amelia peered back at him, her eyes locked on his.

"I still remember this," she said. "Something I always told my kids. Don't make promises you can't keep."

Dr. Reed stumbled backward.

"I'm not," he said. "I promise. I know we can fix this."

But Amelia saw Dr. Jimson, still standing by the door, shaking her head sadly. And she realized something for the first time. These were not gods who had saved her life and promised her all these extra years. They were fallible human beings, practically as confused as she was about what unaging meant. They might or might not be able to restore her lost memories. They might or might not be able to stop her from forgetting more. They would try to guide her and help her, but they were not experts in life, only science—and that had its limits.

Amelia thought back almost ninety years to a day when her four-year-old cousin had fallen into a flood-swollen creek. Amelia and her mother and sisters and aunt and cousins were washing clothes on the rocks of the creek, and Corabelle had wandered upstream, picking wildflowers. Nobody knew she was in the water until they heard her screams. Amelia, who was only twelve, immediately shucked off her skirt and crouched to leap into the creek and grab Corabelle as the water pulled her past.

"No!" Amelia's mother screamed. "Amelia, no!"

But Amelia was already in midair. The minute she landed in the water, it began tugging on her, pulling her downstream. Amelia was a strong swimmer, but her strokes were almost useless. Her head went under once, and then again, but each time she fought her way back to the surface. Blindly she reached out—and touched her cousin's dress. She grabbed it and yanked her cousin's body toward her own. She pushed Corabelle's head above water, but that motion sent her own mouth and nose back down. She gulped in water and choked. With what might have been her last burst of strength, she thrust Corabelle toward the shore. Miraculously, someone caught her. Amelia tumbled in the current again, until her arm caught on a low-hanging tree limb. She held on for dear life, panting and coughing out water. After a long time someone reached out and pulled her back to solid ground. Amelia was too far gone to know if it was an aunt or a cousin or a sister. But she sat up and took notice when her mother ran to her side.

"Mom—" Amelia moaned, reaching out for a hug.

Her mother slapped her.

"You fool! You could have drowned!" Her

mother fell on her knees and wrapped her arms around Amelia's shoulders. "How could you disobey like that?" She slapped her again.

Amelia pulled back, confused. "But I saved Corabelle's life."

Amelia's mother sobbed. "But I didn't want to lose you, too!"

And then Amelia thought that she had got to Corabelle too late, that the little girl had died anyway. But that was wrong, because suddenly Amelia's aunt was there too, hugging Amelia and shrieking, "Thank you! Thank you!"

Corabelle died the next spring of an unknown fever. But the memory of Corabelle's near drowning haunted Amelia for years, most of all because of her mother's reaction. Long after Corabelle had faded in Amelia's mind to a faint memory of a laughing, dark-haired child, Amelia could still vividly recall the feel of her mother's alternating slaps and hugs. Only when Amelia was a mother herself did Amelia understand how confused her mother had been, how proud she was of Amelia's bravery, but how furious at her disobedience, how worried about her life. Thinking back, Amelia realized that that day was the first time that she had doubted either of her parents, that she began to realize that they didn't know everything, weren't perfect.

And now the parents of her second life, Dr. Reed

and Dr. Jimson, were confused too, though they were trying much harder than Amelia's mother had to make her think they were still in control.

Amelia looked straight at Dr. Reed and said, "You don't know anything."

"I always thought the next thing you said should have been, 'Now leave me to my memories, what few I have left,'" Anny Beth said, laughing.

"Thanks. You're more than eighty years late supplying me with a comeback line," Melly said, but she giggled anyway. "Dr. Reed looked stricken enough as it was."

They were reminiscing, something they rarely did. But it was morning now, and they were still in the anonymous hotel in an unknown place, facing an unknown future. Melly thought this was a way to remind themselves who they were and had been. She usually thought she was the only one who needed that reassurance, but Anny Beth had been the one to unleash the flood of memories this time.

She'd been standing at the window, looking at the unfamiliar scenery outside: a few cacti, a narrow road, and sand as far as the eye could see.

"Bill always wanted to live in the desert," she said.

Bill had been Anny Beth's husband for a decade, until he was nearly fifty and Anny Beth was barely thirty. They'd been the same age when they got married. She had never told him about Project Turnabout, and he had never guessed. "But he was going to soon," Anny Beth had explained to Melly the day she left him.

"You are one tough broad," Melly had answered. "Can you quit your husband just like that?"

"Watch me," Anny Beth said, but her voice held none of its usual buoyancy, and she turned her face so Melly couldn't see.

They'd schemed together to get the agency to fake Anny Beth's death, "so at least he won't go mooning around wondering where I went," Anny Beth said. Anny Beth and Melly moved to Minnesota and threw a party the day of her fake funeral. Melly found the "Anny Beth Flick Funeral" Web site on the Internet, but tried to keep Anny Beth away from the computer as long as the Web page was posted.

For her part, Melly had never married this time around—Anny Beth teased her about being a spinster. *Spinster,* of course, was a word that no one used anymore. It was fashionable never to marry in the twenty-first century. Melly wondered about herself—in the twentieth century, when most people got married, so did she; in the twenty-first, when marrying was akin to admitting an affinity for horses and buggies instead of electric cars, she'd followed the trend once again. But she'd been bowing to the restrictions of Project Turnabout, not society. She knew she wasn't strong enough to walk away from a husband she loved, the way Anny Beth had. And what was the alternative?

Now she sat beside Anny Beth looking out into

the desert, wondering about the alternatives for the rest of her life.

"So what are we going to do?" Melly asked.

"Call the agency. We need them to give us fake ID so we can get a new place." But Anny Beth made no move toward her computer.

"You want to move here?" Melly asked without enthusiasm.

Anny Beth shrugged. "Seems as good as anyplace else. There aren't many places left without twenty-four-hour cameras going." For the last several decades every major city—and most minor ones—had had all public streets under constant video camera surveillance, with the tape available at any time from any computer. It had cut crime down considerably, but Melly knew what Anny Beth was implying: If the tabloid reporter knew what they looked like, they couldn't hide in any city.

"Remember when we were in our tour-the-world phase?" Melly asked. When they were in their midsixties the second time around, they both got the travel bug bad. They each circled the world twice. "I said I'd rather live in Timbuktu than anywhere grass won't grow. How could we live here?"

"Want to go somewhere else?"

Melly shrugged. "Where else can we avoid the cameras?"

"Then it's sand, sweet sand," Anny Beth said.

"You live long enough, you're bound to have to eat your words one time or another."

That sounded ominous to Melly's ears. She knew they both needed to get out of this blue funk. "Anyhow, if we're going to find someone to take care of us when we get younger, it'll have to be someone without nosy neighbors to ask why we're shrinking, not growing. We need a hermit. And if there are any hermits left in the world, it'd be in Sky, New Mexico."

Her voice shook, but she went to the computer anyhow and instructed it to dial the agency. The cheery face of the agency secretary quickly appeared on the screen.

"Melly!" Agatha said. "What a surprise! I thought you and Anny Beth only checked in once a year. What gives?"

Melly explained. Agatha's face grew more concerned with each word.

Agatha began punching buttons on her computer before Melly finished her last sentence. "Oh, you've got to come back, then. Let me arrange a flight—"

"No!" Melly said. She could feel her jaw thrusting forward stubbornly. She knew the image Agatha saw on her screen was of a petulant child. She tried to sound mature and decisive, but her voice didn't work that way anymore. "We're fine. We just need new ID. And some way to transfer our bank accounts that can't be traced."

Agatha sighed, but she stopped punching buttons. "I'll talk to the directors and see what we can do. But you know this is very exasperating for them. Why do you insist on fighting the inevitable?"

Anny Beth stepped up behind Melly. "Because coming back to the agency is not inevitable. It's out of the question."

Melly gave her a glance of gratitude. Agatha sighed once more, then said patronizingly, "Whatever you say. Call back tomorrow and I'll let you know the directors' decision. Good-bye."

Agatha's image faded from the screen.

"They're not going to be happy with us," Melly muttered.

Anny Beth shrugged. "They don't have to be happy. They just have to help."

Melly looked out the window, thinking about settling in in this strange place. "We'll have to get them to transfer your college credits, too," she said.

"Yeah," Anny Beth said. "Not that it matters. You know I'm just playing around in college. It's not like I'm going to use this degree for anything."

Melly nodded. She watched the sand blowing in the wind. Now that they were kids again, nobody expected them to be useful anymore. Funny—she'd never realized how much being young and being old were alike. But she still had a big goal, she reminded herself: finding surrogate parents. Surely there was someone here—

Anny Beth stood up and stretched. "I don't know about you, but I'm starved. How about some biscuits and gravy?"

Melly recognized the offer for what it was: comfort food, pure and simple. They'd both eaten biscuits and gravy growing up in Kentucky. Nobody ate them nowadays. Gravy had practically been outlawed after the cholesterol scare of 2010.

"You'll clog your arteries," Melly warned.

"Haven't so far," Anny Beth said.

"Then you'll clog your pores."

Anny Beth's hands flew to her face. "Oh, no—zits!" she exclaimed melodramatically. "I forgot I'd have to worry about those again soon."

Melly nodded, rubbing the small pimple beginning to grow on the tip of her nose. "Now, that's one human affliction I really expected science to cure by now," she said.

"That and the common cold," Anny Beth said.

"And baldness," Melly said.

"And aging," Anny Beth said. When Melly didn't answer right away, she added, "I guess there's still hope."

"For the Cure?" Melly said. "Not in my lifetime."

The words were out before she realized how

meaningful the phrase really was.

"If they came up with another possibility," Anny Beth said, "would you try it?"

"I don't think so," Melly said. "Who'd want to be a teenager forever?"

"People who don't remember what it's like," Anny Beth said. "Peter Pan."

Anny Beth got up and went into the kitchenette. Melly could hear her muttering to the automatic food machine: "Throw in some flour—oh, that's right, you need precision. One cup. And a half cup of milk . . . "

Melly went over and stood in the kitchen door to watch the machine stamp out perfectly round circles of dough, flip them onto a pan, and begin baking.

The biscuits, Melly knew, would not taste anything like what she remembered from her childhood—her first childhood. But they would be adequate. And how trustworthy was her memory, anyway, after 184 years?

"Remember when we believed in the Cure?" she asked Anny Beth dreamily.

"Something like that's hard to forget," Anny Beth snorted.

November 8, 2006

Mr. Johnson wanted it to stop.

"You have the chance to stay any age. Why pick seventy-five?" Dr. Reed argued. "You still have arthritis. You still have wrinkles. You're still bald."

"And I still have most of my memories," Mr. Johnson said so softly that Amelia had to lean in to hear him. Maybe it had been a little too soon to throw away her hearing aid. She'd placed it in the trash can only moments before being summoned to this meeting. The doctors said Mr. Johnson owed it to his fellow Project Turnabout volunteers to discuss his decision, but Amelia thought their true agenda was to have everyone gang up on him and talk him out of it.

"What's a few memories, here and there?" a gruff voice came from the back of the room. Amelia recognized it as one of the other men in the project, Mr. Simon. "You want to be an old man the rest of your life?"

Amelia thought that was a funny question, given that they'd all expected to be old the rest of their lives before Project Turnabout came around. But nobody laughed. Mr. Johnson sat still at the front of the room. He seemed to be staring off into blank space, but then he began answering Mr. Simon.

"My wife died when I was seventy-four," he

said. "I don't want to forget her funeral. Everyone came up to me and told me what a wonderful woman she'd been. . . ."

His voice trailed off. Amelia waited for someone—probably Mrs. Flick—to break the tension with a joke like, "Come on, people say things like that at everyone's funeral. Probably half the people there didn't even know your wife." But the room was silent. All the old people seemed lost in memories of their own—memories they also feared losing.

"Look, we're very sorry about the memory problems," Dr. Jimson said impatiently. "Believe me, we're working as hard as we can to fix that. But this decision would be permanent. In our lab tests, once we stop an animal's unaging, we can't start it again. Trying just . . ." She cleared her throat and hesitated for a second, then went on, more forcefully than ever, "Trying just kills the animal."

Everyone shifted uncomfortably in their seats—all regular chairs now, no wheelchairs. Even the ones who had been in wheelchairs for decades were walking on their own now. Amelia thought it was easier to force yourself to walk when you knew the skill was going to come back. She'd resigned herself to a wheelchair after she broke her hip at ninety-five and overheard the doctor say, "Doesn't all that physical therapy seem like a waste? The therapists will struggle and cajole and kill themselves getting her to walk, and she'll just fall again a month or two later. Or die." So she really couldn't understand Mr. Johnson wanting to give up unaging. Except for the doctors and, now, an occasional nurse or aide, she hadn't seen anyone in five years who wasn't unaging. It was easy to forget that wasn't the natural order of things.

"You fixed the problems of aging," Mr. Johnson said now, stubbornly. "You say you're gonna fix our memories. Maybe you can fix me for more unaging, too. Later. But I can tell you this: You're not going to make me lose anything about Lucille."

"But if you write it all down——," Dr. Jimson started. The doctors had asked all the Turnabout patients to keep what they called Memory Books, to record what they were about to forget. "A temporary measure," Dr. Reed called it. "Like using candles during a power outage." Amelia wondered how much longer he could keep saying that. She had five Memory Books now, one for each year that had disappeared from her mind.

"Writing's not the same as remembering," Mr. Johnson said forlornly.

The doctors exchanged glances.

"Okay," Dr. Reed said gently. "Meeting dismissed."

There were whispers up and down the hallways the rest of that day: "He's going to do it——" "No, he's not——" "Well, I heard he already took the medicine——" "The doctors are trying an experimental memory treatment on him instead." Amelia wondered why the doctors had kept everyone so well informed about everything else but were suddenly so secretive now. Mrs. Flick roamed the halls of the agency, looking for Mr. Johnson, and came back to report, "No one saw him leave the meeting."

Amelia counted squares in her cross-stitch, lost track, and gave up on it. "They'll tell us what happened," she said. "They always do."

Mrs. Flick nodded. "Yeah. If I hear the doctors getting all hepped up about those telly-mirrors one more time, I'm going to croak."

Amelia stuck her needle back in her cross-stitch, guessing at the right place. "Now we're going to have to listen to lots more. Dr. Reed will compare Mr. Johnson's telomeres to all of the rest of ours. Then Dr. Jimson will talk about how his wrinkles won't go away, but ours will, because of all the millions of cells in the skin, which is our largest organ—"

Mrs. Flick laughed because Amelia had mimicked the doctors so precisely. Funny imitations hadn't been part of her pre-Turnabout life. She sometimes had the feeling that she herself would be the biggest surprise of this second chance at life. She took a few more stitches.

"You don't reckon anything went wrong with Mr. Johnson, do you?" Mrs. Flick asked.

"I don't know," Amelia said. "Probably not. Nothing except him making a foolish decision."

But she felt guilty saying that. Roy had died when she was fifty. She had years and years before she would lose any memories of him. So far she'd really lost only the memory of great-grandchildren and great-great-grandchildren she barely knew. She still had pictures. As for her other relatives—the children and grandchildren and nieces and nephews—those she preferred to remember as their younger selves anyhow.

An aide poked her head in the door.

"The doctors are calling a meeting in fifteen minutes in the conference room," she said.

"About Mr. Johnson again?" Mrs. Flick asked.

The aide shrugged. "They don't tell me nothing."

Amelia folded her cross-stitch and stood up, trying to ignore the sick feeling in her stomach. She and Mrs. Flick shuffled out the door together, joining the stream of other people already moving down the hallway. Amelia was struck by a strange desire to join hands, the way she'd held hands with her sisters and cousins on her first day walking to school, all those years ago. Today she stifled the longing for comfort. She wasn't a frightened seven-year-old. She was a woman of the Turnabout. She could handle whatever was going to happen on her own.

When they got to the conference room, Dr. Reed was already standing at the podium. He didn't look up until Dr. Jimson shut the doors and went to stand beside him.

"Everyone is here now," she said dully.

Dr. Reed looked down at the paper in front of him.

"I regret to inform you," he began reading in a monotone, "that Edward Johnson died at one fifty-seven this afternoon. He received an injection of the antitelomerase stimulator PT-2 at one forty-five and apparently suffered a violently allergic reaction. My wife and I offer our condolences to all of you, who are, essentially, his surviving family."

Dr. Reed backed away from the podium, reminding Amelia of dozens of press conferences she'd seen where the president comes in, announces bad news, then leaves before anyone can ask any questions. Dr. Reed, normally so talkative, showed no inclination to say any more.

He had already turned his back on the crowd before a voice rang out.

"Now, wait just a cotton-picking minute!" one of the women yelled. "You can't just leave it like that! Why didn't it work? What went wrong? Is that what's going to happen to the rest of us?"

Dr. Reed stepped back to the podium. He leaned into the microphone and whispered, "I don't know."

Hysteria broke out then. People screamed, "But

you have to know!" "How could you let this happen?" "But Mr. Johnson believed in you—"

Dr. Jimson rapped on the podium until the hubbub subsided enough that she could make her voice heard.

"Silence!" she screamed. "Silence. Don't yell at us! PT-2 worked on mice. It worked on monkeys! We had every reason—well, almost every reason—to expect it to work on Mr. Johnson. We didn't know—"

"But you're supposed to know—," someone hollered.

Dr. Jimson hit the podium again.

"We can't know everything!" she screamed. Amelia watched in amazement. *She's going to cry. Dr. Jimson, the ice queen, is going to cry.* But Dr. Jimson didn't. She swallowed hard and seemed to regain her composure.

Still, her loss of control momentarily shocked the crowd into silence. That gave Mrs. Flick an opening to say, in a perfectly calm voice, "Then maybe Mr. Johnson isn't dead."

Everyone turned to stare at her. She went on.

"Maybe it's just a coma. Like before," Mrs. Flick said. "Remember? You all thought we died after the first shot. But you were wrong. Maybe you're wrong now."

"No." Dr. Jimson was shaking her head wildly. "No. You don't understand. You'd have to see—"

"We've got to show them the video," Dr. Reed said in a hollow voice.

Dr. Jimson turned to stare at him. But for once he was a few steps ahead of her. He was already turning the TV toward the crowd and hitting buttons on the remote control.

The picture that appeared on the screen was of Mr. Johnson sitting in this very room. His shirt-sleeve was rolled up, and Amelia could see the swath of orange antiseptic already swabbed on his arm. Dr. Reed and Dr. Jimson both hovered over him.

"I'll ask you one last time," the Dr. Reed on the screen said in a patient voice. "Are you absolutely certain this is what you want?"

"One hundred percent," Mr. Johnson replied, his voice ringing with confidence.

"Okay," Dr. Reed said doubtfully. He picked up a syringe and eased the needle into Mr. Johnson's arm. He pushed on the syringe, and the yellowish liquid inside disappeared into Mr. Johnson's arm.

"Feeling all right?" Dr. Jimson asked.

"Just fine," Mr. Johnson said. But his face had already begun to change before he said the second word. His cheeks went hollow, his eyes bulged, his jowls drooped. His body hunched over. He was aging. Rapidly. Amelia looked over at the untelevised Dr. Reed to see if he had hit the fast-forward button on the remote. But that was crazy, because even fast-forward couldn't condense decades into seconds. On the screen Mr. Johnson shriveled further, faster. Amelia almost felt relieved when his head dropped forward, obviously in death. At least it was over for him.

The televised Dr. Reed and Dr. Jimson could only stand back in horror.

The real Dr. Jimson rushed to her husband's side and grabbed for the remote.

"For God's sake," she shrieked. "Don't show them everything!"

She stabbed a finger at the remote and the TV screen went black.

"His body disintegrated," Dr. Reed mumbled, as if in a trance. "Into dust. Right before our eyes."

Dr. Jimson slapped her husband.

Chaos broke out in the room once more. People screamed and sobbed and pleaded. The doctors made no effort to restore order.

Amelia sat still and silent, so numb she barely noticed when a chair hit her in the leg. People were throwing things? Somehow it made sense to her. This was a horrible shock. This wasn't Louise Swanson killing herself because of her son's betrayal. This was Mr. Johnson getting the cure they all planned to get someday, and having it kill him. She'd spent the last five years believing she was virtually immortal now—they all believed that. She'd never realized how much that had changed her outlook on everything. How could she believe in her own mortality again? Did she have to? Couldn't the doctors fix PT-2?

She didn't realize she'd spoken the question aloud until Mrs. Flick answered, "You mean the way they fixed our memories? Hey, stop that!"

Amelia turned and saw that Mrs. Flick was fending off a crazed man flailing his arms at everything and everyone in sight. Finally the melee around her registered with her eyes and ears. In the front a gang of men had advanced on the two doctors and were pounding on their backs, screaming, "How dare you! You lied to us!" Another group was trying to stop the first, with cries of, "Don't hurt them! They're our only hope!"

Amelia blinked in astonishment. How could all the others be acting like this? They were old. Old people took bad news sitting down. They swallowed all their hopes and dreams and fears and nodded off toward death.

Except she was wrong. The people around her weren't old anymore. Neither was she. Sure, they'd all lived a long time, and they still sported the white hair and wrinkles and bald pates that marked them as elderly. But part of being old was knowing you were near the end. And none of them did. None of them were. That's why they'd reacted to the news of Mr. Johnson's death like teenagers in a riot.

Amelia stood up, steadying herself with one hand on the arm of the chair. She looked with pity at Dr. Reed and Dr. Jimson. But there was nothing she could do to help them.

"I have to leave," she said to no one in particular. She walked out of the conference room, closing the door firmly behind her. Then she went to her room to pack.

Melly and Anny Beth lay flat on their backs in the sand, peering up at the night sky. The stars wheeled over their heads. Melly picked up a pebble and threw it as far as she could toward the moon. The pebble went straight up, then plopped back into the sand a few yards away. In spite of her problems, in spite of the uncertainty, something about the sound of the falling stone made Melly feel good. Maybe it was just those crazy teenage hormones coursing through her veins. Or maybe it was just life. After almost two hundred years perhaps she'd learned to appreciate it. She took deep breaths of the clean desert air.

"Do you ever wonder what our lives would have been like if we'd never left the agency?" she asked Anny Beth.

"No," Anny Beth said. She propped herself up on one arm and drew waves in the sand with one finger. "It would have been eighty more years of the same thing. Meetings twice a day with the doctors. So much talk about telomeres that our brains would glaze over. Constant gossip about, 'They've almost fixed the memory problem,' 'The Cure will work the next time.' We'd spend all our lives wondering whether or not we were going to be able to live forever."

Melly threw another pebble at the sky. "It was the other people I had to get away from," she said. "More than the doctors. If I were only around others who were unaging, I would go crazy."

"Thanks," Anny Beth said. "Want me to leave now?"

"You're different," Melly said. "You don't dwell on things."

"Whatever," Anny Beth said. Her waves in the sand turned into circles, then swirls. "But I thought you were crazy that day you said you were leaving. I'm glad you talked me into coming along."

"Remember that form they made us sign? How many ways can they make you say, 'I will not contact any of my family, go anywhere that I might be recognized, or take my story to the media'?"

"Well, there were about two hundred clauses on that form. So about that many times," Anny Beth replied.

Neither of them talked for a few minutes, and Melly could almost make herself believe they were just ordinary teenagers hanging out looking at the sky. (Did ordinary teenagers do that anymore? she wondered. They had the last time Melly was fifteen.)

"I could get to like this place," Anny Beth said. "Puts me in mind of Kentucky."

"What?" Melly asked. "Let me remind you:

Kentucky has trees, grass, and mountains. All this place has is sand. I feel like I'm in the middle of nowhere."

"And that's how I felt in Kentucky. When I was eighteen—the last time, I mean—I hated that so bad."

"So you should hate this, too," Melly said.

"Nah, there's no such thing as being nowhere anymore. All you need is a phone line, and you're connected to the whole world."

"That's what I'm afraid of," Melly said, and shivered, thinking of the tabloid reporter again. Once the agency gave them new ID, she wouldn't have to worry anymore. Would she?

They heard the phone ringing back in their hotel room.

"Let the computer get it?" Anny Beth asked.

"No, it might be Agatha."

"So?"

"We need to be nice to her, especially right now. And remember all those job applications we put in today? It may be someone calling for an interview."

"Can't we play hard to get?"

Melly was already opening the sliding glass door. She hit the switch on the side of the computer that turned it into a speakerphone.

"Picture?" the computer asked. Melly didn't want any potential employers thinking she was paranoid, but she hesitated. She hit the button for caller ID. The words scrolled out on the blank screen: *Caller: A. J. Hazelwood.*

Shaking, Melly quickly typed in the command for the computer to ask for a message.

"Hello?" A woman's voice filled the room. "My name is A. J. Hazelwood, and I'm trying to reach Amelia Hazelwood. I believe we are distant relatives, and I'm trying to track down some family information. I'd appreciate it if you could call back at—"

Melly didn't stay around to hear the number.

"Anny Beth!" she shrieked out the door. "It's that reporter!"

Anny Beth raced inside just in time to hear the message click off. Melly played it back for her.

While Anny Beth just stood there in shock, Melly began typing in numbers. "I've got to call the agency. They have to get us fake ID right now!"

Anny Beth put her hand over Melly's to stop her. "No, wait. Let's think about this."

Melly stopped typing, but she was too scared to think.

"How did she find you again?" Anny Beth asked.

"She saw satellite pictures of our car's license plate. She called up the hotel registration or the credit transfer records. You didn't hide anything."

"Well, you can't," Anny Beth said defensively. "The computers detect fraud instantly. And it's not like I could have paid cash. But those records are like state secrets. Nobody can get to them unless they're authorized."

"Maybe she is."

"No." Anny Beth shook her head violently. "Reporters are the last people who would be authorized. It has to be something else—"

"Maybe it's that E-mail postcard I sent Mrs. Rodney—'Gosh, I wish I were still baby-sitting for you instead of lying in this sandpit,'" Melly said sarcastically. "Come on, Anny Beth, you know we didn't tell anyone where we were."

"Yes, we did," Anny Beth said slowly. "We told the agency."

Melly stood still, trying to figure out what Anny Beth meant.

"You think the agency turned us in?" she asked. "You think they're out to get us?" It was a thought that never would have occurred to her on her own. She thought of the people at the agency as misguided, not malicious.

Anny Beth sank to the bed and buried her face in her hands. After a moment she looked up at Melly. "I don't know," she said miserably. "What other explanation is there?"

Melly gritted her teeth, thinking. "Maybe this A. J. is just a really good hacker. Maybe she broke into our records—"

"With the government? Come on, the government's had antihacker protection for seventy-five years."

"Then, at the agency?" Melly trembled as she made that suggestion. If the reporter had access to the agency's computer records, she knew everything about them. Their private lives were over. "Wouldn't they have antihacker protection too?" It was strange, the number of things she didn't know about the agency. Once she'd left, she tried not to look back.

Anny Beth threw up her hands helplessly. "It doesn't really matter, does it? Either the agency spilled the beans on purpose, which means we can't trust them, or your darling descendant is so brilliant she figured out how to get information from them without them knowing it. Either way, we've got to hide from the agency."

Melly sat down beside Anny Beth and stared bleakly out the window. The desert scene beyond looked even more desolate than before. Hiding from the agency would mean no fake ID, no help at all. She'd spent the last eighty years thinking she was independent of the agency, but that wasn't true. She'd always known she could rely on the agency officials, if worst came to worst. It was like still having a family, but one that you rarely saw because Aunt Mildred drove you crazy and Uncle Arnie was an embarrassment. But now, if they cut off contact with the agency, they would truly be alone.

"We could go back," Melly said quietly. "Or just me. I'm the only one she's after. Then you could do whatever you wanted."

"You'd go back to the agency?" Anny Beth said. She launched herself off the bed and began pacing the floor. "Is that what you want?"

"Of course not," Melly said. "But—"

"No buts," Anny Beth said firmly. She began hitting the wall at each end of her pacing: Two steps, hit! Two steps, hit! Then she whirled around to face Melly. "There are two problems with that plan.

First, it doesn't solve anything. You go back to the agency, it just makes it easier for the reporter to track you down. And it guarantees that all the other Project Turnabout people will be exposed too."

"Oh," Melly said weakly.

"And second, it leaves me on my own. Listen, I've been married four times. The first three times were pretty much duds—at least that's what I wrote down when I remembered them. The fourth time, with Bill, was great. He was the best husband anyone could ever have, and I loved him like crazy. But even when I was married to him, the person I counted on the most was still you. You've kept me in line for eighty-five years. What would I do without you?"

Tears blurred Melly's eyesight. Anny Beth had never said anything like that to her before. She'd never had to.

"Okay," Melly said. "I feel the same. We're in this together, no matter what. But what should we do? Where do we go? Would—" A new thought occurred to her. "Could you go back to Bill?"

She thought about how strange that would be—Bill's one-time wife now showing up as his grand-child. Could Bill and Anny Beth adjust to such a different relationship? Would Melly want to have to watch them try?

"No," Anny Beth said evenly. "Bill died right after I did."

Melly hadn't known that. They'd had the same policy with Bill that they had with most things from the past: It's better left unspoken. She thought about the way Anny Beth had phrased that announcement. "Bill died right after I did." It was a revealing slip of the tongue, maybe proving that Anny Beth felt the same way Melly did about the different portions of her life: that she really had been different people at different times. She thought about some of the dopey books she and Anny Beth had read about adolescence when they were trying to fit in. "Adolescence is a time of finding your identity." It was such hogwash. Even in the first half of Melly's life, which had been dead ordinary, she'd had many identities: daughter, sister, wife, mother, grandmother, great-grandmother. This time around she'd been a virtual change artist. The question was, What should she change into next?

Melly turned to Anny Beth, who was staring, clear-eyed, out the window.

"All right," Melly said. "There's no one we can go stay with. We've just got to find someplace so remote neither the reporter nor the agency would find us there. And we've already eliminated the most godforsaken place I've ever seen." She pointed out the window.

"I know what we have to do." Anny Beth spoke as if in a trance. "We've got to go home."

"Home?" Melly asked, puzzled. She thought of

all the places they'd lived in the past eighty years. It was a list of practically every state in the country. Every state but one. Melly began to understand. "You mean—?"

"Yes." Anny Beth's voice was solemn. "We'll go to Kentucky."

Just the word, *Kentucky,* brought back a flood of memories for Melly of her first childhood, of hard work and hard play and loving family around her. *Yes*, she thought with a rush of longing, *that's where we belong*. But she knew it wasn't possible.

"Anny Beth," she said, "there's a story I never told you. . . ."

MARGARET PETERSON HADDIX

The depression hit when Amy was forty-four. For weeks she filled her journals with her misery: *I take no pleasure from my life anymore. I forget to eat. I can't sleep. What's the point?* Anny Beth had just got married and was in a state of newlywed bliss with Bill. Amy told herself she wasn't jealous, and she really wasn't. She'd had a perfectly happy marriage herself, the first time around, and it was easy in the twenty-first century to be happy without a spouse. She liked Bill well enough but didn't want him or anyone else for a husband. No, what she wanted was a baby.

How can my biological clock be ticking? she wrote. *This is ridiculous. My best years of fertility lie ahead of me. If I wanted to, I could get pregnant ten years from now, even twenty.* But she stared at babies in stores, sometimes even reaching out to touch their little curled fists before their parents snatched them away, frightened by the strange woman with the longing look in her eyes.

She had never tried to find out any extra information about unaging, beyond what the agency told her, but now she began some surreptitious research. She sat up late at night, surrounded by computer printouts, and made notes on old-fashioned lined paper with antique pencils:

CAN I HAVE A BABY?

1. *I probably have no more eggs. They're one of the things, like teeth, that don't come back with unaging.*
2. *But if I wanted to, I could go to a fertility specialist and have him inject my DNA around some other woman's egg. They do that nowadays. And I could have artificial insemination.*
3. *Would I be able to carry a baby to term? Probably not. My body goes backward, not forward. Surrogacy is outlawed, but they have artificial wombs now. It seems unnatural, but still—*

She paused and looked at the words she'd written in her early-twentieth-century script: *Fertility. DNA. Insemination. Artificial wombs.* Crazy words that should have nothing to do with having a child. She'd never even heard of such things the last time she had babies; anytime during the first half of her life most of the words on that list would have made her blush violently. She crumpled the paper and threw it across the room. She swept all the computer printouts onto the floor, then stuffed them into the trash. "You're wrong!" she yelled into the emptiness of her house. She'd been looking at "Can I have a baby?" as a biological question. It wasn't. It was a moral one.

She grabbed her journal and scrawled, *Can I*

have a baby? Of course not. It's not fair to any child to have a mother who's unaging. We'd have to keep so many secrets. And if the worst happened—if the media found out about me—her life would be ruined too. And when I unage all the way, when I'm four and two and then just a baby—how could she look at me and call me Mom?

Amy cried for days, devastated at the thought of never having a family again. She hadn't ever realized how much she'd held out hope for that. She wouldn't marry, she wouldn't bear children—in her first hundred years those had been the things that mattered. How could she find significance in anything now? She began watching the tabloid TV shows, taking notes during all the "ordinary-people exposés" of what people valued in their lives: Hot computers. Sharp cars. Good food. Great sex. Money. Easy jobs. She took to shouting, as feistily as Anny Beth, at the TV screen, "You fools! Your lives are nothing!"

And then one morning, while she lay in bed preparing to cry again, a new idea came to her. She needed to start over. If she retraced her steps and went back to Kentucky, where she'd lived practically her entire first life, surely she could get her life back on track. She'd find meaning once again.

She began thinking of the journey as a religious pilgrimage. If she could just look out on the

Appalachian Mountains once more, she'd understand what God wanted her to do with the rest of her life. There was one particular spot, not far from where she'd grown up, where you could stand on a peak and reach for the clouds, an entire valley at your feet. She needed that place.

She scoured video maps and satellite maps and travel tapes, and discovered, to her overwhelming relief, that her special place was still there. It hadn't been bulldozed to make way for a Wal-Mart Universal store. It was protected wilderness. There was even a quick view of her spot in the computer video archives, though she resisted looking at it for very long. She didn't want a virtual pilgrimage. She needed the real thing.

The agency called the day before she was ready to leave. They were trying out a robot receptionist.

"Ms. Hazelwood," the robot said in its emotionless monotone. "Your birthday is next week. It is time for your annual checkup. When shall I schedule the appointment? You have not been answering your E-mail."

Amy hadn't even been looking at her E-mail.

"Sorry," she apologized automatically. Then, because it was just a robot, she added recklessly, "I'm going on a trip to Kentucky. I don't know when or if I'm coming back. So I'll call you about that appointment. I'll let you know."

The robot's head began spinning around, red lights flashing and buzzers blaring. "Emergency! Emergency!"

"What did I say?" Amy asked. Before anyone could answer, she panicked and cut off the connection. She stared at the computer for a full minute before she realized what must have happened: They'd programmed the robot to respond to the word *Kentucky.* They'd think she was violating her promise never to go where anyone would recognize her. But she hadn't been back to her hometown in more than fifty-five years. Anyone who remembered what she'd looked like at forty-four—the first time around, a hundred years ago—had died long ago.

She looked nervously out the window, as if daring someone from the agency to come and stop her. She paced, considering leaving early. But she'd sent her electric car to the shop for a checkup and to receive a maximum recharge before the trip. If she wanted to leave now, she'd have to take public transportation or buy a new car. She decided to wait.

At eight o'clock the next morning, an hour before she was supposed to pick up her car, the doorbell rang.

Amy sat still at her breakfast table, willing whoever it was to leave.

"Mrs. Hazelwood!" a creaky old-woman voice called out. "Please let us in!"

Being called Mrs. Hazelwood once again was all it took. She quickly crossed the room and opened the door.

The most ancient-looking couple she'd ever seen was standing on her doorstep. The man held a cane but still clutched the woman's arm as though his legs could never get enough help. The woman looked none too steady herself, all shriveled and shrunken into a fragile little gnome.

"Mrs. Hazelwood?" the man croaked in disbelief.

Amy gave a half nod. "And you are . . . ?"

"Dr. Reed," the man wheezed.

"Dr. Jimson," the woman whispered.

Amy couldn't help it: She gasped. She did some quick math in her head: fifty-seven plus—what? Thirty-five? Forty? The doctors were both at least ninety years old.

"You never took PT-1 yourselves," she said.

"No." The man shook his head, a process requiring such intense effort that Amy found it painful to watch. "And we never will."

Amy squinted, trying to see in these ancient creatures some glimpse of the doctors she remembered from a half century ago. Something about the eyes—did eyes change? These people's eyes were bleached out, ghostly. Maybe eyes did change. Or memory did. When she'd been old, just about all she'd noticed about the doctors' appearance was their youth and vitality. And now that she was younger, all she saw was their age.

"You've unaged quite nicely," Dr. Reed said in his eerie rasp.

"I guess." Amy shrugged helplessly. Somehow it seemed too cruel to accost the doctors with any of the angry accusations that had been running through her mind lately. *Why did you have to keep me alive this long? I'm a freak of nature—what am I good for?* Instead she invited them in. They took long, slow steps and spent a good ten minutes easing themselves down into Amy's living-room couch.

Amy perched uneasily on her least comfortable chair.

"Why?" she finally blurted. "Why won't you take PT-1? You don't have to live like this."

"No," Dr. Reed agreed. "But we saw—" He looked to his wife, and in that motion Amy recognized him. So some things never changed.

"We decided unaging was wrong." Amy could tell that Dr. Jimson wanted to speak as firmly and confidently as ever, but her voice wasn't up to it. She went on. "You and Mrs. Flick are about our only success stories. That we know of."

Amy debated telling them how successful she'd been feeling the last few weeks, but didn't.

"But the others—," she protested.

"A few have disappeared," Dr. Jimson said.

"They left and cut off all ties with the agency. Several have committed suicide." She fixed Amy with an unflinching stare, which Amy recognized as well. Dr. Jimson's philosophy of delivering bad news was like giving a shot: Do it quickly and get it over with. "Others have begged for the Cure, and that still is not effective."

Ah, Amy thought, *so Dr. Jimson has discovered euphemism in her old age.*

"And the rest?" Amy asked, shivering suddenly. "The others who stayed at the agency?"

"They are physically healthy." Dr. Jimson appeared to be choosing her words carefully. "But they are not pleasant people to be around."

"Oh," Amy said.

"Either they are obsessed with unaging," Dr. Reed said, "or they are obsessed with the past and the memories they are losing. And that is why we have come to beg you not to go to Kentucky."

Amy blinked, not quite sure how they'd got from the others' problems to her own.

"Pardon?" she asked.

Dr. Reed began tapping his cane on the floor.

"You can go," he said. "We can't stop you. And—" he raised his hand to stop Amy from protesting— "I know you can argue that you're in no danger of being recognized. You will not be violating any of the promises you made when you left the agency. But when you get down there, it's going to be too tempt-ing for you. You'll want to start reliving the past. You'll want to look up all your descendants and find out what happened to them. You'll find some way to ingratiate yourself into their lives. And it won't be natural. It isn't natural for you to be younger than your great-grandchildren. We messed around with nature, and we shouldn't have. We've left you in a painful position, and you would very likely hurt your descendants too. Because before very long you'd have to tell someone. And then people talk." He paused and chose another angle for his diatribe. "From what we've seen, the best way for unaging people to live is for the present and the future. Not the past. You've been working as a preschool teacher, right?"

Amy bit her lip, thinking of all the children she'd taken care of in the last decade. Other people's children.

"Yes," she said. "But I'm on leave. I . . . I can't do that anymore."

"Then do something else," Dr. Jimson said. "Something like that, that makes a difference in the world."

Stubbornly Amy looked away. She pictured once again the scene she wanted to return to: the glorious mountains, the gentle valley.

Dr. Reed sighed.

"You're not convinced," he said. "I suppose you

don't have to be. I'll put it this way: Even if you don't understand, humor an old man. Please. I know what I'm talking about."

Amy flushed, suddenly angry.

"I'm older than you are," she said bitterly. "I'm one hundred and fifty-six. Remember?"

"Yes," Dr. Reed said softly. "But you're also forty-four."

Amy didn't answer right away. One hundred fifty-six or forty-four—they were just meaningless numbers. She'd been alive longer than Dr. Reed. If he was going to pull that older-and-wiser shtick, she had the upper hand. She glared at Dr. Reed, prepared for another angry outburst, but his gaze stopped her. His rheumy eyes almost looked through her, as if seeing his death waiting near. She remembered that look from long ago, from her first lifetime, when she'd tended her dying mother. She remembered her mother struggling to say, "Death . . . does . . . focus . . . the mind. . . ." Those were the last words she ever spoke. Amy had been forty-two then, and hadn't understood.

"All right," she told Dr. Reed now. "I won't go."

Strangely, she and the doctors had nothing to say to one another after that. They were gone before nine o'clock. But instead of rushing to pick up her car, Amy went to her computer and typed in, *"Midlife career change. Search."*

And the next morning when the agency robot called to say that the doctors had been in a terrible car wreck, and both died, Amy accepted the news without the slightest bit of surprise.

"Well," Anny Beth said when Melly finished her story. "I guess that explains those fifteen years you spent as a hospice nurse."

"Yep," Melly said without looking at her friend.

"You could have told me," Anny Beth said. "I didn't know you were sad when I married Bill."

Sad was such an old-fashioned word. Nobody in the twenty-first century was ever sad—they were depressed, emotionally unbalanced, incorrectly medicated. Sorrow was a disease that everyone rushed to cure. Melly was strangely glad, suddenly, that she'd spent all those weeks wallowing in her misery more than twenty-five years before.

"I was happy for you," Melly tried to explain. "But for myself—"

"You needed to be around dying people to make yourself feel better?" Anny Beth joked.

Melly nodded, all seriousness. "I worked the night shift, remember? And I'd leave every morning, sometimes still covered in vomit and excrement and the stench of death, and I'd step out on the porch and look at the sunrise, and it was like . . . being born again, or something. I'd think, 'I get hundreds more sunrises. I'm alive!' I felt so lucky just to have another day, when those poor people were dying. . . ."

Anny Beth didn't laugh, the way Melly had

expected her to. She drew her legs up close to her body, perched her elbows on her knees, and leaned her chin on her hands. She peered back at Melly. "So you took that part of Dr. Reed's advice and it worked—it helped you to help other people. And now you think he was right that you shouldn't go back to Kentucky?"

Melly shrugged. "I promised."

Anny Beth sprang off the bed and began pacing once more. "Why is it that for the first half of my life I couldn't find a single honest person to hang around with? My relatives, my husbands, my friends, my kids—all of them would tell a lie as easily as they breathed, and not think a thing of it. A promise was like . . . like spit, something you made and got rid of and didn't worry about. And now— now when I really need to lie and break promises— I'm stuck with the only moral person in this whole dang century."

Melly couldn't help it. She laughed.

"You make me sound so strange," she complained.

Anny Beth sat back on the bed. "You are. Because a promise you made almost thirty years ago to someone who had no way of knowing what you'd be facing now should not stop you from doing anything."

Melly lay back on the bed and stared up at the ceiling.

"It doesn't matter," she said in despair. "We can't hide in Kentucky anyway. Without the agency we can't get any new ID, so we won't have social security numbers, so we can't work. We've both got money in the bank, but the agency could probably trace it every time we made a withdrawal. Let's face it—we can't survive without the agency."

Anny Beth was shaking her head violently. "Didn't you say some of the other Project Turnabout people cut off contact with the agency? They must have figured out how to survive on their own."

"Or not," Melly moaned. "They probably all ended up dead in some back alley somewhere."

Anny Beth gave her a playful tap on the shoulder. "Quit that," she said. "Think positive. Some of them had to have figured out how to get their own ID, how to take care of themselves. They had to have adapted. Some of them must have survived."

Melly groaned, not convinced. "Well, the only way I know how to survive on my own is with a wood-burning cookstove and a well and plenty of flour sacks for clothes. In this century—forget it."

She closed her eyes, waiting for Anny Beth's sarcastic reply, but it didn't come. After a minute Melly opened her eyes and looked over at Anny Beth.

Anny Beth was staring off into space, her mouth agape, her eyes wide.

"What?" Melly asked.

　　　　　　MARGARET PETERSON HADDIX

"You're absolutely right," Anny Beth said. "Melly, you're a genius! That's how we can hide!"

"How?" Melly said, mystified.

"By living the way we know best," Anny Beth said. "By giving up this century."

PART THREE

April 25, 2085

It's 3 A.M. Anny Beth and I have been talking for hours, trying to figure out if her plan will work. Now she's sacked out on the bed. That's one of the things I've always hated about her, that she can stop in the middle of anything—a fight, a conversation, a movie—and declare, "I'm tired," and instantly go to sleep. I won't be able to sleep for hours, if at all, for thinking about all this.

It's crazy. Even Anny Beth admits that. Sure, we both still remember how to live without computers and automatic cookers, or even electricity and running water. But we sure don't want to.

Anny Beth keeps saying that I shouldn't see this as a permanent plan. She thinks we can hide our car and our computers somewhere and go back to them occasionally. She says this is just buying us time. And right now we do need time to find out how the reporter traced us here, to find out if someone in the agency is out to get us, to figure out how to get away from the reporter once and for all. And then . . . to find someone to take care of us. No matter how worried I am about us now, I can't forget that problem too.

I know, if we stay here, the reporter could easily come here—in person—to find us. And someone from the agency is supposed to call back tomorrow, *and we have to believe that anything we tell the agency might get back to the reporter. . . .*

The easiest thing would be to give in and do what Anny Beth wants. She's so sure of herself. But I can't forget the promise I made Dr. Reed not to go back to Kentucky. It was twenty-eight years ago, and I couldn't foresee this, but still. Isn't a promise a promise?

I argued with Anny Beth that if the point is to live in the wilds, we could live just about anywhere there's still some protected space. The American Northwest is still beautiful, and now that we're already in New Mexico, it's actually closer. But Anny Beth says I'm forgetting how hard it is to survive in wilderness. We know what plants are edible in Kentucky. One wrong bite in the Cascade Range could kill us. I guess she's right about that.

The thing is, when I think about breaking my promise to Dr. Reed, I think that I might as well go whole hog and break other promises too. Because it occurs to me that maybe the best people to take care of me when I get younger are my own kin. And where else am I going to find them but in Kentucky?

They arrived at the woods near Quicksand, Kentucky, just before midnight. Anny Beth hid the car in the trees, and they both stepped out, inhaling deeply.

"Oh, Anny Beth," Melly sighed. "It still smells the same. Just like I remember, all that pine . . . and the stars are so bright—"

Anny Beth snorted. "More like, you're seeing the glow of the Wal-Mart Universal parking lot on the other side of the preserve."

"Oh." Melly looked at Anny Beth questioningly.

"I looked it up," Anny Beth said. "I had to do something while the car was on autopilot and you were asleep. I memorized all the area around here."

Melly frowned. "Can anyone trace us through the autopilot?" she asked.

"I hope so," Anny Beth said. "Because the car has lots of miles left to go tonight. We can't keep it here longer than it would take to make a pee break."

"I thought we were going to keep the car—"

Anny Beth shook her head grimly. "And have the license plate spotted by satellite? We can't risk that."

"But you said that reporter wouldn't have access to satellite records—"

"No, but I got to thinking—what about the agency? If they've had enough access to change our

IDs every year, couldn't they get into other government records? And if the reporter is getting information from the agency . . ."

Anny Beth didn't have to finish her sentence. Melly shivered. She felt like she was traveling in a maze—wasn't there some route that didn't lead to the monster in the middle?

"Aren't you going to help?" Anny Beth asked. Melly realized Anny Beth had begun unloading the bags of flour, sugar, and salt. She dropped a particularly heavy load right at Melly's feet. "I can't do everything around here, you know."

Anny Beth's indignation was just the prod Melly needed. She followed Anny Beth and grabbed the boxes of milk. Better to do *something* than sit around worrying. After just a few minutes they had everything out that they needed. Anny Beth leaned over the steering wheel and double-checked the programmed coordinates.

"Wait," Melly said. "My Memory Books . . ."

She pulled out her two big boxes, one of her journals since the year 2000, and one of the books full of memories that now existed only on paper.

"Won't be fun carrying those uphill," Anny Beth said. But she, too, leaned back into the car and pulled out two boxes.

Melly gaped. "I didn't know you kept those," she whispered.

Anny Beth shrugged. "Under this stunning physique I'm just a sentimental old lady. Just like you."

Then she pressed the button that sent the car on its way alone. Melly and Anny Beth watched until its laser license-plate glow disappeared over the next rise, a mile down the road. Melly felt a threat of panic at her throat. Without the car their only means of escape would be on foot.

"Where'd you send it?" she asked

"Back to our old house. So it'll look like we just went on a quick around-the-country vacation."

Melly snorted, wondering how gullible someone would have to be to think they'd been on vacation.

"There's a cave, up this hill—," Anny Beth began.

Melly squinted into the darkness of the woods ahead. "I know," she said quietly. "My brothers and sisters and I used to play there."

Pine branches rustled in the breeze, and for a second Melly could imagine it was one of her sisters playing hide-and-seek. "A-meal-yuh! Come and get me!" echoed in her head, and she stepped forward, as though she truly expected to find Gemima or Liza Mae or Ray Lee or Joe behind the tree. But it'd been almost two centuries since they'd been children; they'd all died and been buried in the cemetery on the other side of the ridge decades before Melly had begun her turnabout. She suddenly missed them all again with an intensity she'd rarely felt in the last century. She bit her lip, willing herself not to cry. So this was why she wasn't supposed to come back to Kentucky.

"Earth to Melly," Anny Beth said. "You gonna help me, or stand there mooning the night away?"

Melly saw that Anny Beth had pulled almost all of the boxes behind a tree. She was piling the rest of the supplies into two backpacks.

"Doesn't this make you feel at all nostalgic?" Melly asked.

Anny Beth turned to face her squarely.

"Kentucky," she said, "is where my stepfather beat me once a day, minimum. Twice, if the dog wasn't around to kick too. And where he left off, my husbands took over. So, in a word, no."

"So you've been running away from this for the past eighty-four years," Melly said, waving her arms to indicate the woods in front of them.

"I prefer to think that I've made my peace with the past and moved on," Anny Beth said stiffly. "We've both been to enough psychology classes to know it could be interpreted either way."

Melly remembered that Anny Beth had got a Ph.D. in psychology several decades ago.

"Still," she said. "Is this going to be too hard on you?"

Anny Beth shrugged. "What's done is done. You're the one who had a problem with coming here."

To show that she wasn't suffering from second thoughts, Melly picked up one of the backpacks and thrust her arms through the straps. She watched Anny Beth do the same.

"You first," Anny Beth said. "You know the way."

They started hiking up the hill. Once they passed the first few trees, the path broadened enough that they could walk side by side.

"You left the computers in the car, didn't you?" Melly said.

Anny Beth nodded. "I'm pretty sure they could be traced too. You know, one of us should have taken a few years out to study computer technology or advanced hacking, instead of all that social science."

Melly thought of the degrees they held: social work, psychology, sociology, nursing, education. Nothing that would help them defend themselves against a tabloid reporter.

"Everybody else in this century knows all the computer stuff. I figured we could always ask," Melly said. "We'll have to find a public library."

"What for?"

"We need to find out if there's already anything

on-line about us. And we need to investigate our descendants to find someone who will take care of us when we get too young."

Melly waited for Anny Beth to protest. Instead she said, "I wondered how long it would take you to reach that conclusion. You're breaking promises right and left today, aren't you?"

Melly shifted the pack on her back. "Morality just isn't as easy as it was the last time I was fifteen," she mumbled. "I've thought and thought about this. I even prayed. I think this is the right thing to do."

Mercifully, Anny Beth didn't challenge her again. They walked in silence in the moonlight for almost a mile. Then the path split and Melly hesitated.

"You go on that way and I'll catch up," she said. "I just want to see something—"

"No, let's stick together," Anny Beth said.

They walked around a curve and through the trees and stepped into the clearing. And there, in the moonlight, stood the house Melly remembered. She'd once thought it impressive—huge compared with the shacks many of their neighbors lived in. But after all the years she'd spent living in electronic splendor, with all the luxuries of the twenty-first century, this place seemed like a rustic cabin. The wooden walls were bare brown, the windows unadorned, the porch plain concrete. Melly dropped her backpack and stood and stared, soaking in the sight.

"Someplace you recognize?" Anny Beth asked.

"Where I was born," Melly said. "Where I grew up. Home."

Anny Beth was kind enough not to say anything for a long time.

"Could we stay here?" Melly asked. "It'd be better than the cave—"

"Maybe someone's already there," Anny Beth retorted.

"In protected territory? And look, there's no smoke from the chimney."

"There wouldn't be," Anny Beth said. "Wood-burning fires were outlawed fifty years ago, remember?"

"I forgot," Melly murmured. Being back in Kentucky had somehow thrust all her memories of the current century far to the back of her mind. But she latched onto a sudden concern. "Oh, no—how are we going to cook?"

Anny Beth sighed. "I brought a portable cooker," she said. "I had to rethink the idea of roughing it. We can't hunt, we can't have fire—living in the past is really impossible now."

Melly wasn't sure exactly how she meant that. "But we can still stay here," she said. "Not because of nostalgia. It's more practical." She reshouldered her backpack and prepared to step forward.

Just then the door of the house opened and the

porch light came on. A dog ran out, followed by a young woman.

"Go on, you silly mutt," the woman yelled good-naturedly. "But hurry back. Why can't you learn to go before bedtime?"

The dog yelped in response and scrambled down the porch stairs. Melly and Anny Beth simultaneously slid behind the nearest tree, out of sight. It didn't matter. The dog ran right toward them, sniffing deeply. He stopped at Melly's shoes and began barking. Melly froze in fear.

The woman on the porch laughed.

"Leave the raccoons alone, you idiot," she called. "Want to get us kicked out of the preserve? Now, do what you have to do and come on back."

The dog gave three more barks, then evidently decided that if his mistress didn't care about intruders, neither did he. He galloped back toward the house.

Melly allowed herself a sigh of relief. While the dog was still cavorting around, making a huge racket, she and Anny Beth turned and ran from the house.

"So much for that idea," Anny Beth said when they reached the main path once more.

"It's not fair," Melly complained. "That house should be mine." For some reason she couldn't get the image out of her head: a stranger on the porch of her home.

"After one hundred and eighty-five years you still expect life to be fair?" Anny Beth asked. But she put her arm comfortingly around Melly's shoulders as they walked toward their cave.

April 26, 2085

Melly woke early the next morning. Cave floors were not the most comfortable places to sleep, even with high-tech sleeping bags to cushion the rock. And even though she was quite tired, there was a song repeating itself in her brain all night, it seemed: "Get up, get up, find out what's next—" The sun was barely over the horizon when she stepped over Anny Beth's sleeping form and tiptoed to the cave's entrance.

The rays of pink and blue shot across the sky, like so many exclamation points over the tops of the budding trees. The cave was near the peak of the mountain, so Melly could look down on miles and miles of unspoiled woods. She summoned a mug of hot chocolate from the automatic cooker and sat on a rock to drink it with the full vista of wilderness at her feet.

"Who wouldn't want to live forever in a place like this?" she mumbled to herself. But she didn't have forever, and there was too much to take care of right now to just sit around enjoying the scenery. She gulped down the rest of her hot chocolate and instructed the cooker to make bread for breakfast. Then she headed downhill to bring up the rest of their things from the hiding place beside the road.

Just as she carried the last box up the hill—

MARGARET PETERSON HADDIX

panting, because all those Memory Books were heavy—she heard a scream from inside the cave.

"No! Leave me alone!"

Melly dropped the box on the path and rushed in to find Anny Beth thrashing in her sleeping bag. Her skin was clammy and her hair was plastered to her head with sweat. Melly grabbed her by her shoulders and shook.

"Anny Beth! Wake up! Are you having a nightmare?"

Anny Beth fought her off at first, knocking Melly against the cave wall. Then Melly got a firm grip on Anny Beth's arms. Anny Beth's eyes slowly focused on Melly.

"Oh," she said. "It's you. I was dreaming—"

"Your stepfather?" Melly asked.

Anny Beth nodded weakly. "But when I've dreamed about him before, he's always stronger than me. . . . I always lose. This time he was little and I was big. I beat him up. I threw him across the room. I really think I'm okay now." Anny Beth's face shone with triumph and sweat.

"Yeah, well, you threw me, too. Now, can you help me clean up this blood?" Melly showed Anny Beth the gash on her arm.

"I'm sorry," Anny Beth said. She reached for their first-aid kit and expertly dabbed at the wound with Speedy Healer. They both watched the ragged edges of the cut close up into a faint pink line. Anny Beth started giggling. "I'm sorry. But if it was you I threw, no wonder my stepfather seemed so light and easy to beat."

"Hey, anytime you need help overcoming psychological traumas from the past, call on me," Melly said. She hesitated. "So, he was big?"

"Six three, probably three hundred pounds. Known for miles around as the meanest man in the state. I never had a chance against him."

"I'm sorry," Melly said. "Isn't it strange that, as long as we've known each other, we've never talked about him before?"

"No," Anny Beth said. "Since the turnabout, we've had different lives. Now maybe we're melding them together."

It was the most philosophical statement Melly had ever heard from Anny Beth.

"Should we?" Melly asked quietly.

Anny Beth shrugged.

They made their plans during breakfast. Anny Beth agreed to hike to the nearest library, which she calculated to be about six miles back up the road.

"It's safer for me to go than you," she explained. "No reporter's looking for me."

"But surely this reporter has figured out that we're together. . . ."

Anny Beth took a huge bite of bread, chewed, and swallowed before answering.

"I'll be six miles from our hiding place. I don't expect to be there more than this once. And what other option do we have?"

Melly nodded slowly, not wanting to agree. Really, she wanted to be at the library too, getting the information at the same time as Anny Beth. "But what'll I do while I wait?"

Anny Beth washed her bread down with hot chocolate, draining the mug and placing it back on the rock they'd been using as a table. She stood up and stretched.

"Hey. I guess you get to relax."

It was a laughable notion. Melly put a ridiculous amount of effort into cleaning up after breakfast. She picked crumbs from the rock as though expecting some Sherlock Holmes to come around looking for hints of any human presence. A squirrel upset at the lost chance for food *chee-cheed* a scolding.

"Oh, leave me alone," Melly grumbled back.

She carried all the boxes into the cave and made sure their sleeping bags and other supplies were as far back from the entrance as possible, hidden from any passers-by. She didn't really expect any: Visitors were rarely allowed into protected lands. Technically, she and Anny Beth were violating dozens of environmental laws. That was why she was surprised that anyone was living in her old home.

The memory of the woman standing on the porch of the old house—*Melly's* old house—kept coming back to her. So when she'd finished every chore she could possibly think of, she found herself heading down the trail toward the house. The sensible thing to do would be to hide until Anny Beth returned—all the wisdom she'd gained in her long life told her that—but there was no way she was going to sit alone in the dark for an entire day. What teenager could?

In daylight the house looked different: smaller, darker, more run-down. Hiding in an enormous forsythia bush that hadn't existed in her last lifetime, Melly squinted through leaves and wondered how much the house had changed in the past century, compared with how much her memories of it had changed. It was her home—she knew that—but she didn't feel the same emotional pull of the night before, when shadows and darkness had hidden all the changes.

Still, Melly watched with great interest when the woman stepped out on the porch again, calling back to the dog, "No, you silly mutt, you've got to stay home this time. And don't wear yourself out barking at the squirrels through the window, you hear?"

Now that Melly got a better look at the woman,

she could tell she was fairly young—Melly guessed late twenties, early thirties at the most. She had small features, short, light brown hair, and a jaunty swing to her stride. She reminded Melly of someone, but as Melly thought back through all the people in all the places she lived, she couldn't think who.

The woman started down the hill in the opposite direction from the cave. Without thinking, Melly started following her, stepping carefully to avoid attracting attention. One of their neighbors when she was growing up had boasted that in his youth he'd served as a scout for the great Daniel Boone himself. The neighbor, Mr. Craven, had gone so far as to show Melly's brothers how to creep silently through even the densest brush, as if that proved his wild tales to be true. Melly and her sisters had laughed at the boys' mincing steps, their anguished winces at every cracking twig and rustling leaf. But secretly the girls had practiced too, and Melly had somehow mastered the trick of putting down her feet without placing her full weight in any one spot. It was something about the swaying of her hips— maybe that wasn't the way Mr. Craven did it, but that was what worked for her. Somehow the skill came back to her now, as she followed the woman from her old house.

When she was a kid—the last time—Melly and

her brothers and sisters had always pretended to be hiding from Indians. Sometimes when they miscalculated their steps and accidentally made a huge ruckus, they'd clutch their hands around the imaginary arrows sticking out of their chests and cry, "Oh, no! He got me!" One of her sisters, Liza Mae, had been good at dramatic death scenes too. Now, of course, Melly knew children no longer played that Indians were the enemy. All the textbooks had been rewritten, and Columbus Day had been turned into a national Day of Atonement, an annual time of apologizing to Native Americans. Melly understood the reasons and mostly approved, though she kind of missed the simplicity of the past. Even now what she feared was not clear-cut and definite—like death—but entirely abstract. If the tabloid reporter found her, if her secret was exposed to the world, she'd go on living. It would just be a miserable existence.

Melly was so busy thinking that she got sloppy and snapped a twig. Melly quickly crouched, hoping the undergrowth would hide her, but the woman in front of her didn't even turn around to look. Perhaps she was lost in thought too.

After a mile or two the woman began veering downhill. The woods changed too. Melly tried to remember why everything suddenly seemed so unfamiliar, then realized—this had been Dry Gulch, the nearest town. Melly's family had come here to shop just about every Saturday morning. And now all the stores were gone, along with all the houses, all the roads, all the cleared land. Melly could see no trace of the past.

Melly briefly considered stopping and looking more closely, in memory of all the people who'd once lived here. But what was the point? She kept following the woman.

At the bottom of the hill Melly could see that the woods ended. The woman stepped out onto blacktop. Melly slid downhill, suddenly worried that she'd lose track of the woman. Melly landed on the blacktop several paces behind. Without the trees around her the glare of the sunlight was blinding. She had to squint and let her eyes adjust before she saw where the woman had led her: a Wal-Mart Universal store.

"Guess this proves Anny Beth knows how to read a map," Melly muttered.

By now the woman was practically on the other side of the parking lot, nearly up to the door. Without stopping to analyze why it was important to keep up with her, Melly took off running. She heard the screech of brakes but didn't have time to react. An automated shopping cart slammed into her leg.

"Ow—" Melly crumbled in pain.

"Watch where you're going!" The man driving

the cart didn't seem to feel a smidgen of guilt or compassion. His wrinkled face was twisted in an expression of disgust. "Kids! Think you're going to live forever, so you endanger everyone else! I could have got whiplash!"

Melly straightened up and decided nothing was broken, only bruised. As the pain ebbed she wanted to giggle. Oh, if only the man knew how far she was from believing she would live forever.

"I'm sorry, sir," she said in the most polite voice she could summon up without laughing. "I'll be more careful next time."

She walked away, chuckling to herself at the man's drop-jawed astonishment. She hoped she'd never been that kind of bitter old person.

The woman from her house was in the store now, totally out of sight. Melly rushed in through the vacuum doors, but her cause was hopeless now. The woman could be in any one of a hundred aisles. Melly could search all day and never find her. She walked up and down the aisles anyway.

After just one night in the woods the sights and sounds of an ordinary store were overwhelming. All those bright colors, the brand names shouting from the shelves—no wonder most people avoided nature nowadays. The reintroduction into civilization was too jarring.

Feeling dazed, Melly closed her eyes, trying to

MARGARET PETERSON HADDIX

adjust to only one sensation at a time. Sound first. Voices swirled around her: A mother scolding a child, "Suzie, keep those hands to yourself!" An elderly woman asking someone, "Would you kindly reach that box on the top shelf for me?"

Melly smiled, able to hear more with her eyes closed than open. There was still a twang in these people's voices that sounded like the Kentucky she remembered. She thought back on all the news stories she'd read over the past half century explaining that TV and the transient nature of American lives had finally killed all regional accents, all regional differences in speech and thought. But those stories had been wrong. She could still hear home.

She opened her eyes and looked around. Was it her imagination, or did the stock boy getting the box from the top shelf have the same jutting jawline as all the Lawsons who'd lived down the mountain from her family growing up? Wasn't the little girl in the shopping cart—probably Suzie of the wandering hands—a dead ringer for Pearl Gaines, who had been one of Melly's playmates in grade school 170-some years ago? These people had to be the descendants of the people Melly had known, so long ago. The families had lived on, even if the individuals hadn't. Melly felt the resemblances were a gift; a part of her that had gone numb over the disappearance of Dry Gulch felt much better.

Then she turned around and saw the woman from her old house. This was her lucky day.

The woman was buying dog food. Melly followed her at a distance as she also picked out a box of computer disks and threaded her way to the checkout counter. While the woman emptied her cart for the price scanner, Melly ducked into a checkout line labeled OUT OF SERVICE and pretended to examine the rows of candy and gum. She absentmindedly fingered a pack of gum that promised day-long bubbles while she watched the woman over the top of the rack.

The woman's computer screen flashed the total, and she swiped her debit card across the sensor. Then Melly got the reward she'd been waiting for: The screen flashed *Thank you, Ms. Hazelwood* in response.

Hazelwood! So she had to be some relative of Melly's!

As foolish as she'd felt for following the woman before, Melly felt entirely justified now. She couldn't wait to tell Anny Beth that she'd found something out today too.

Melly had only two seconds of feeling triumphant before the buzzers started going off around her.

"Warning! Warning!" a voice boomed around her. "Shoplifting suspect in line fourteen!"

Melly gasped and looked around. She was in line fourteen. She was the shoplifting suspect. How could she have been so stupid, drawing attention to herself like that? She knew that the surveillance cameras were programmed to set off alarms over suspicious behavior. And lingering over a candy rack was suspicious. Well, she'd just have to buy the gum. She said aloud, "I'm planning to pay for it."

The alarms stopped. But as she reached into her pocket for her debit card she remembered: No, she couldn't pay for it. Not without announcing to the whole world exactly where she was.

Melly looked around cautiously, contemplating throwing the gum to the floor and dashing out of the store. The surveillance cameras would memorize her image and probably track down her identity by comparison to some international data bank of surveillance tapes anyhow. Running would only increase the chances that she would be found out.

Melly moved to the back of a long checkout line, hoping that would give her time to come up with a better plan. The woman from her old house—Ms. Hazelwood—glanced her way once, without much curiosity. Then she picked up her dog food and computer disks and began walking for the door.

Melly advanced in her line, in agony. How could she be the one to blow her own cover? How could she be so stupid?

She was next at the computer. Resignedly she dug deep into her pants pocket, pulling up her debit card. And then—something else. Paper. Money.

Melly pulled the green strip up as though it was an artifact from another time. She stared at it stupidly for an entire minute before she remembered: This was what she'd been paid for baby-sitting—or, truly, not baby-sitting—for little Logan Junior, back when Mrs. Rodney had told her about the reporter calling. Melly had crammed it in her pocket and forgotten about it in the rush of fleeing, first from home and then from the hotel. But these were the same pants she'd been wearing that day.

Melly breathed a silent prayer of thanks that even in the twenty-first century parents still sometimes paid teenage baby-sitters in cash. She stepped up to the checkout computer and inserted her cash into the dusty hole at the top. The letters on the computer screen blinked slightly, as though the computer were stunned to get anything but a debit card.

"You paid fifty dollars for a two-dollar piece of gum," the computer informed her. "Do you expect change? You must go to the service desk for that. Or shall I credit the amount to your debit card?"

If she hadn't feared arousing more suspicion, Melly would have let the computer keep her forty-eight dollars and been done with it. But she meekly trudged over to the service desk and filled out the form—in triplicate—explaining why she deserved cash back.

The man behind the counter searched in vain for something to give her.

"You'll have to wait until we call the bank and ask for a delivery," he explained. "Are you sure you left your debit card at home? Can't you go back for it?"

"Okay," Melly said with fake enthusiasm. "That's a great idea! That's what I'll do!"

He wanted her to leave her name, but she talked him into giving her a receipt instead. It didn't matter. By the end of the conversation he was staring at her so suspiciously that she knew he'd be reviewing the surveillance tapes anyhow.

She slunk out of the store and back into the woods feeling totally disheartened. She'd been stupid, yes, but there was just no way to hide in this world. Probably there were surveillance cameras somewhere in the woods that had captured video of Melly and Anny Beth entering and leaving the preserves. Probably someone was already searching for them, to arrest them. No wonder crime was so low nowadays. No wonder nobody understood the word *privacy* anymore.

Back at the cave Melly crawled into her sleeping bag. There was nothing she could do until Anny Beth got back. She just had to hope that Anny Beth got back before someone came to arrest her.

April 27, 2085

Melly was dreaming about playing chase with her brothers and sisters when she felt someone poking her in the side.

"Hey," came Anny Beth's welcome voice, "it's not fair that I had to walk twelve miles and work all day while you did nothing but sleep!"

Melly didn't bother correcting her. She sat up quickly, wide awake. "What'd you find out?"

Anny Beth handed her a thin electronic pad. "I downloaded everything into that. Believe me, you and I have spawned a load of exhibitionists. We can pick out people to take care of us based on belly button size if we want."

Melly winced.

"Of course, it's going to take us a year or two just to read all of that," Anny Beth continued.

"We don't have that kind of time," Melly muttered. "Did you find out if the tabloids have anything about us?"

Anny Beth shook her head. "There's nothing in print. And of course all the records of what they're working on are off-limits. They probably protect their files better than the government protects military secrets."

Melly turned the electronic pad's switch to "on" and asked for an index.

"Did you find out anything about the reporter? A. J. Hazelwood?" she asked Anny Beth.

"Is there anything to eat?" Anny Beth said instead of answering. "I'm starving."

Melly pointed to the portable cooker.

"Darn. I thought you'd have a gourmet meal waiting for me," Anny Beth said. She began punching buttons on the cooker. Melly marveled at Anny Beth's ability to focus on basic needs—food, sleep—regardless of anything else. It was probably that survival instinct that had accounted for her long life. The first half of it anyway. Only when the cooker was whirring away did Anny Beth turn back to Melly. "What'd you ask?"

"About the reporter," Melly said patiently. "What did you find out about her?"

"Funny thing," Anny Beth replied as she lifted a synthesized turkey dinner from the cooker. "She's the only private descendant you have. There's almost nothing on her except the public records a person can't prevent from being on-line."

Melly called up the file marked *"A. J. Hazelwood."* Virtually every line Melly clicked on said, *"Access denied at request of subject."*

Melly squinted in confusion at the screen.

"Why?" she asked Anny Beth. "Why would anybody do this?"

"Ever check what's on public record for the two

of us?" Anny Beth countered.

"No," Melly said.

"Not much more than that," Anny Beth said. "And almost all of it's false except our names."

Melly shrugged, not interested in discussing their own decisions just then. "Did you find out anything else?"

"A little." Between bites Anny Beth showed Melly what to click on. "She did work as a reporter, but it was just for a local Web site, not anything national. From the looks of the stories she did, the only exposés she had were about corrupt sewer boards and politicians who spent their money on gold-plated faucets in the statehouse restroom when they were supposed to be helping underprivileged kids. Nothing sexy."

Melly stared at the list of headlines in front of her: *"Committee Funds Misappropriated," "Congressman Smathers Denies Budget Flaw," "Funds Held Up in Political Debate."* In spite of herself Melly had to smother a yawn.

"Very old-fashioned of her," she muttered. "But I don't get it. Why's she after me? I don't see a single 'Two-Headed-Baby-Born-in-Iowa'-type story anywhere."

Anny Beth chewed thoughtfully. "Maybe she just wanted to get to know her great-great-great-grandmother."

Melly rewarded Anny Beth with a frown and kept scrolling through the list. "Wait—there's not a single story after September of last year."

Anny Beth leaned over the electronic pad. "Hmm. You're right. I didn't notice that. Maybe they fired her for being too dull. Hey, did I walk twelve miles to find surrogate parents, or to investigate the person who's investigating you? Come on, you know you don't want that reporter as a parent."

With a sigh Melly clicked back to the main menu. "Right now I'm not ruling out anyone."

The next time Melly looked up, Anny Beth was sound asleep, her head slumped against the rock. Melly hunched over the electronic notepad and kept reading. *"Annabel Hazelwood,"* she read. *"Orthopedic surgeon . . . Chest size: 46D . . . "* Well, that would fit. Must be one of her grandson Dexter's grandchildren. According to the Memory Books, he'd married a woman who was ridiculously over-endowed. Melly looked down at her own fifteen-year-old nearly flat chest and decided she shouldn't be prejudiced just because this Annabel had something she didn't. *"Firm believer that astrology has been overlooked as a cause of recent human events . . ."* Now, that Melly could be prejudiced against. She zapped Annabel off the screen and went on to Anga Hazelwood. Melly read with growing amazement Anga's list of interests: *"Waterskiing, parachuting, parasailing, scuba diving, ecology, rain forest revitalization, native people's justice, soothsaying, creative anachronism, computer Zen, virtual prehistoric travel . . . "* Life with Anga would certainly never be dull. Then Melly belatedly noticed Anga's birth date. She was only thirteen. Oh, well.

For the next several hours Melly crept through descriptions of mechanics and millionaires, sport fishermen and religious zealots, ordinary computer programmers and extraordinary entrepreneurs. With some entries she felt a thrill of pride: "This is one of my descendants!" On others the feeling was abject shame: "How could my blood be beating through the heart of a serial killer?" Most of the people she found seemed fairly normal—for the twenty-first century, anyhow—and potentially good surrogate parents. But how could she be sure? These people had publicized everything about themselves; there was so much public information, Melly kept trying to read between the lines for some hint of the private individuals. But maybe there was nothing more to them. Maybe they had no private thoughts, no private selves.

Melly had only got as far as Harold Hazelwood when she stood up and stretched and went to the front of the cave to watch the sunrise. Unlike yesterday— had it only been yesterday?—this morning she sat and watched the whole extravaganza from beginning to end, from the first faint glow on the horizon to the whole ball of sun, fully hatched, too bright to look at. She was still staring off into the distance when Anny Beth crept out beside her and handed her a plate of food.

"Bet you didn't eat all night," Anny Beth said.

"No," Melly said vaguely, and absentmindedly took a bite of synthetic eggs. "Too much to do."

She took another bite and chewed in silence. Anny Beth wasn't much of a morning person, so Melly knew not to expect a lot of chatter. After a long while Melly asked, "Did you watch many sunrises the last time you were a teenager?"

"Nope," Anny Beth said. "I was a sunset type of kid. Always believed dusk was when the excitement started."

"Yeah," Melly said. "I used to love sunsets too. And I remember right after we left the agency, eighty years ago, I went through a sunset fixation. But if my Memory Books are believable, I loved sunrises when I first went in the nursing home. And I love them now."

"There's no mystery to that," Anny Beth said. "People crave what they don't have. When you were at the beginning of your lives, you were fascinated by endings. And one hundred years ago you thought you were nearing the end, so you liked beginnings. And now—"

"Things are ending again," Melly mumbled. "What is that, Psychology 101?"

"No, that's from my doctorate studies," Anny Beth bragged. "And you thought all those social sciences we studied were useless."

Melly rolled her eyes. She took a deep breath.

"I found a surrogate parent for us," she announced.

Anny Beth looked over at her expectantly. "Oh?" she said. Melly could tell she was forcing herself to sound casual. "Anyone I'd know?"

"Actually, yes," Melly said. "Sort of. It's the reporter. A. J. Hazelwood."

Anny Beth laughed without much mirth. "Very funny. Who is it really?"

"I'm serious," Melly said quietly. "I've been thinking about it all night. She's the only one who isn't in the habit of telling everything she knows to the entire world. She's the only one who could keep us secret."

Anny Beth frowned. "But she's a reporter! She—" Anny Beth stopped, finally considering the suggestion seriously. Melly waited patiently, as though Anny Beth were a computer working through a complicated problem.

"Okay," Anny Beth said finally. "Your logic is twisted but not entirely insane." She rubbed her forehead wearily. "Still—we don't have to do anything right away. Let's hang low for a while. Think some more. We've got, I don't know, years before we'll need someone taking care of us. We can line up our first and second and third choices, maybe spy on them to check them out. Then when we're absolutely sure, we can spring our little surprise."

If there hadn't been so much at stake, Melly would have laughed at the role reversal: Usually she was the one urging caution, Anny Beth the one ready to follow any impulse. But Melly didn't feel much like laughing right now.

"We don't have years to make a decision," Melly said. "I'm not sure we even have many more hours." Briefly she told Anny Beth what had happened the day before at the Wal-Mart Universal.

Anny Beth punched a rock in frustration. "Ow! Melly! How could you have risked blowing our cover like that? Are you sure you're not just being paranoid? You paid for the gum—they're not going to try to track you down just because you don't show up to get your change."

"I don't know," Melly said. "I know they were suspicious. They probably are checking up on me. And anyhow—don't you think there are satellites watching these woods? Someone's probably on their way to arrest us right now."

Anny Beth grimaced. Melly could tell she didn't want to admit Melly was right.

"It just won't work," Melly went on. "You just can't hide out in this century. The only reason we could keep out of the tabloid Web sites before was that we had the agency helping us. How many records and tapes do you think they had to erase and doctor? If we don't go find a surrogate parent now, we'll probably be arrested by nightfall. And when they check us out, either the agency's going to have to rescue us again—if they can—or our secret's out." Melly heard her voice go high and squeaky near the end, like a little girl begging for help.

Anny Beth buried her face in her hands.

"Okay," she finally muttered. "You've convinced me." She rubbed her temples hard and looked up at Melly in despair. "But if you're sure that reporter's the person we want, we've got another problem. Her address is classified. We don't even know where she lives."

"I do," Melly said, shooting a look of triumph at Anny Beth. "She lives in my old house."

For a long time Anny Beth could only gape at Melly.

"How . . . how do you know?" she finally sputtered. "Are you sure?"

Melly bit her lip. "Well, not one hundred percent," she admitted. "But it makes so much sense—"

"I think I'm missing something, then," Anny Beth said. "You'll have to explain it to me."

Melly used her fork to draw designs in her eggs. Was she right? What if she convinced Anny Beth and was wrong?

"This is someone who writes about sewer boards and financial appropriations and political scandals that don't involve sex. She's obviously longing to live in the past. So what do you do when you want to live in the past? You move back into your ancestors' house and live the way your great-great-great-grandparents lived."

Anny Beth shook her head. She stabbed some of the eggs on her plate with unnecessary force. "Psychologically speaking, maybe you're right. But that's just a guess. We need to be one hundred percent sure."

Melly crumbled her toast and threw it out into the woods. She wasn't worried about detection now. It felt good to throw something.

"Come on, Anny Beth," she said. "You've been

alive for one hundred and eighty-seven years. Haven't you learned that nothing's one hundred percent sure?"

Anny Beth gave Melly a long look. Then she abruptly stood up.

"Okay," she said. "Let's get this over with."

She started walking down the hill but stopped after a few steps to look back over her shoulder. "Aren't you coming?" she called back to Melly.

After eighty-five years Melly should have been used to Anny Beth's split-second decisions. But she couldn't help sitting still for a while longer, totally stunned.

"What are you waiting for?" Anny Beth repeated.

"I—there . . . there's something else you should know," Melly stammered. "Something else that makes A. J. Hazelwood the right person to take care of us."

"Oh?" Anny Beth said impatiently. "What is it?"

"She's your great-great-great-granddaughter too."

"What?"

"One of your great-great-granddaughters married one of my great-great-grandsons. A. J. Hazelwood is their only child."

Anny Beth started laughing. "You're kidding! Some of our descendants actually mated? And someone related to me managed to stay out of jail?"

"Jeez, Anny Beth, one of your descendants is president right now. You've got a whole branch of incredibly rich and famous—and, by all accounts—morally upstanding descendants. That's the only reason I know about A. J.'s parents. One of her cousins was really into name-dropping, and traced the entire connection on her Web pages."

By now Anny Beth was laughing so hard she could barely stand up.

"It can't be," she gurgled. "President?"

"Yep." Melly got carried away by Anny Beth's laughter. "And you know Riley Standish—the woman they call the Mother Teresa of this century? The one who ended starvation in the third world? She's one of yours too."

Anny Beth had to sit down after that one.

"This is too rich," she said between peals of laughter. "All these years I thought I'd unleashed a pack of liars and cheats and murderers on the world. Why do you think I did all that social service all those years? I was trying to make up for my offspring—dang! I could have been out partying!"

Melly couldn't help laughing at that.

"I don't know," she said. "There are probably some murderers among your descendants too. I know I had some."

That only made Anny Beth laugh harder.

"I don't care what happens to me now," she said.

"My life is complete. I know now that I spawned a saint and you spawned a murderer. Hey—race you down the hill."

Anny Beth had a head start, but Melly dashed after her.

They were like that the rest of the way to Melly's old house—giddy, loud, exuberant. It was as if, having finally made a decision, they felt free, regardless of how things turned out. They crashed through the brush, not caring who heard or saw them. Melly had run that way through these woods a million times with her brothers and sisters, all those years ago. All she needed was to dash up the porch steps and bang the front door and she'd feel entirely, completely at home.

But when they got in sight of the house, both of them stopped. Suddenly deadly serious again, they froze by the forsythia bush Melly had hidden behind the day before.

"Got any plans for breaking this to her?" Melly whispered.

"Want to go for the shocker? 'Hi, we're two of your great-great-great-grandmothers. We just happened to be in the neighborhood and decided to stop in for tea.' How's that sound?" Anny Beth whispered back.

Melly shook her head no.

They peered through the leaves at the house.

The windows were open, and white lace curtains blew in and out. Otherwise everything was still. There were no signs of either the woman or her dog.

"Well, we can't wait forever," Anny Beth proclaimed. She grabbed Melly's hand and pulled her to the door. Melly looked for an automated doorbell—of course there wasn't one. Meanwhile, Anny Beth had the presence of mind to knock.

"Hello?" she called in through the screen. "Anyone home?"

The dog came running to the door, barking. Then the woman appeared out of a back room. Melly held her breath.

"Down!" the woman commanded, and to Melly and Anny Beth's amazement the dog dropped obediently to his paws. His barks turned into a whimper, and then he was silent.

The woman came to the door. "Yes?" she said.

Melly forced herself to exhale. Then inhale. "Are you A. J. Hazelwood?" she asked.

The woman nodded, looking puzzled. Through the screen door Melly could see how small her features were, how her light brown hair waved in the same place as Melly's own. Suddenly Melly realized who the woman reminded her of: herself. The way she'd looked only fifteen years ago.

"I'm Melly," Melly announced. "Amelia."

The woman's puzzled look only deepened. "Do I

know you?" she asked. She looked out at Anny Beth. "Or you?"

"Maybe," Melly said softly. She made herself breathe in and out carefully. This had to be the right thing to do. It had to. "You were looking for me," she added.

Something like comprehension started to come over A. J.'s face, then she looked confused again.

"Amelia Hazelwood," Melly said.

"I was looking for someone a little, uh—"

"Older?" Anny Beth supplied the word.

A. J. nodded. "I must have made a mistake. I'm sorry. Did you come here just because—"

"We had a lot of reasons," Anny Beth said. "We'll explain if you promise this is all off the record."

Melly was glad Anny Beth remembered to say that. But A. J. frowned.

"I'm sorry," she said, almost frostily. "I don't believe there's any information I need from you. So there's no reason to grant off-the-record protection."

"Now I know why she failed as a journalist," Anny Beth whispered to Melly. "No nose for news."

"I did not 'fail' as a journalist," A. J. snapped back. "I'll have you know I've won two Pulitzer Prizes for public service."

"Is there any competition in that category anymore?" Anny Beth taunted. "Only the tabloid news category means anything now."

"But—" A. J. clearly couldn't argue that point. She switched tactics. "Anyhow, I didn't 'fail.' I quit to write a book."

Melly and Anny Beth exchanged glances.

"What's it about?" Anny Beth asked.

"I don't believe that's any of your business," A. J. said calmly. "Now, if there's nothing you can tell me on the record, I need to get back to work. And you should leave before the police show up to arrest you for trespassing on protected lands. In the future if you need to contact me, please do so by E-mail or telephone."

She turned around, as if expecting them to leave. Melly felt her stomach clench into knots. This was not working right. She looked appealingly at Anny Beth. Anny Beth seemed to be thinking.

"She's got an honest face, don't you think?" Anny Beth asked quietly.

"What are you talking about?" Melly asked. "She's got my face."

"That's what I mean," Anny Beth said. Then she hollered after A. J.'s retreating back. "Wait a minute. At least listen to what we have to say. Then you'll understand why we want this off the record. And if you understand, then you'll give that to us. Okay?"

"Why should I agree to that?" A. J. replied without turning around.

"Because"—Melly took a deep breath—"because

you may find this hard to believe, but we're really two of your great-great-great-grandmothers. And we didn't exactly stop in for a cup a tea."

A. J. turned around. And in the same moment a voice behind them shouted, "Freeze! Department of Protected Lands here! I have a warrant for your arrest!"

Melly's heart sank. How could the police have caught up with them now, just when they'd told A. J. the truth?

"Officer," Anny Beth said calmly. "I'm sure you know from your weapon scanners that we aren't armed. Could we turn around and face you?"

"All right," the man replied.

Anny Beth leaned over and whispered to Melly, "Sure beats the old days when they had to frisk you."

While they all waited for the police officer to cross the yard and mount the porch steps, Melly expected A. J. to fade into the background, perhaps even shut the door. She'd warned them to leave before the police came—surely she was feeling a little triumphant that they'd got what they deserved.

But A. J. shot them a compassionate glance and stepped protectively to the front.

"What are the charges in that warrant?" A. J. asked.

Melly watched the officer's face as he fumbled with his handheld computer. He was young, possibly not even twenty yet. Patrolling protected lands must not be considered difficult duty.

"I have to identify all parties present for a legal hearing," the officer said apologetically. "Are you"—he read A. J.'s name off the computer screen—"Annabeth J'amelia Hazelwood?"

"Can you believe it? She's even named after us!" Anny Beth whispered to Melly. Melly shot her an annoyed look. Names hardly mattered at the moment. Then Melly realized A. J. had heard Anny Beth too. A. J. peered at Anny Beth thoughtfully for a moment, then turned her attention back to the officer.

"You know who I am," A. J. said. "You come and sign my permit every week."

"Yes, yes," the officer said, even more apologetic. "Got to do things by the book."

"The charges?" A. J. reminded him.

"Oh, yes." The officer looked back at his computer. "Satellite footage showed that these two— infrared photo identified as Amelia Hazelwood, age fifteen, and Anny Beth Flick, age eighteen—entered these protected lands illegally two nights ago. Does either of you dispute these charges?"

Melly opened her mouth to say something—or maybe just to beg for mercy—but A. J. spoke for them.

"How can they?" she asked. "When are satellites ever wrong?"

"Well, just between us and the trees, ma'am, the satellites have been on the blink the past week or so because of storms over Siberia. That's why it took us two days to download the info about these two. Normally we'd've had them within an hour—"

Melly had never thought in her long life that she'd feel grateful for storms over Siberia, but she did now. Still, the storms hadn't bought quite enough time for her and Anny Beth, because they hadn't had a chance to tell A. J. everything. A. J. glanced at them, her expression unreadable. Melly looked down, her mind racing. What next? Would they end up in jail? Would they be allowed to contact the agency? Would they have to?

"I'm sorry, sir," A. J. was saying. "I don't mean to cut you off, but we're in the middle of a rather delicate family situation. These girls are distant relatives of mine, and they didn't quite understand the law. But I told them their actions were illegal, and they're sorry. Could you tally up their fine on your Portable Court and let them go?"

"They'll have to buy a permit, too—," the officer warned.

"Fine," A. J. said.

Melly slid her hand into her pocket, as if reaching for her debit card, but she was only buying time. If she used her debit card, the agency would be able to find out where she was—even she knew court fines were public records. All her instincts told her to run, to go hide until she found another relative she wanted to live with—someone sane enough not to live on protected lands. But those were her twentieth-century instincts. If she ran now, the satellites would track her every move.

Before Melly had a chance to decide what to do, A. J. had pulled out her own debit card.

"I'll pay," she said. "It's my fault they're here."

Melly watched in amazement as the officer zipped A. J.'s card through his computer and gave her a receipt.

"Have a pleasant family visit," the officer said. "And remember, if they perform any more illegal actions—"

"You can hold me responsible," A. J. said.

As soon as the officer had walked away and was out of earshot, Melly turned to A. J. and exclaimed, "Why did you do that? Did you really believe what we told you?"

"That you're my great-great-great-grandmother? Give me some credit!" A. J. said with a laugh. She peered out at the woods to make sure the officer was gone. Then she opened the door to let Anny Beth and Melly into her house. "I figure this is going to be so ridiculous it might be worth listening to. And I'd rather hear your story before the police do."

Melly frowned, wanting to believe that A. J. had been motivated by something more than curiosity.

All three of them sat down in the front room. Melly recognized some of the furniture: an armoire her father had made, a chair her mother had rocked all her babies to sleep in, years and years and years before. Seeing the furniture was almost as heartrending as if she'd walked in and found her mother and father right there waiting for her. She had to stifle the impulse to go over and stroke the grain of the wood. *If only—*, she thought, and for once let herself finish the thought. *If only she hadn't promised the agency not to see her family. She would have been with this furniture all along. It was true, she would have seen all the descendants she knew die, but she would have known their children and their children's children. . . . She would have known A. J.* Now Melly could just hope A. J. was the right person.

A. J. sat straight in her Shaker-back chair. Everything about her body language seemed to say, "I'm waiting. Don't you have something you were going to tell me?" Distantly Melly wondered if that was a reporter's trick, something journalists learned in school to get people talking. Probably not. In this day and age people needed no encouragement to start talking.

"Well?" A. J. said expectantly.

Melly and Anny Beth exchanged glances.

"This isn't exactly easy to explain," Melly apologized.

"No, I wouldn't think so," A. J. said. Melly couldn't tell if she was making fun of them or not.

Anny Beth broke in. "Look, we've never told anybody this story. We have to be sure we can trust you. Can't you tell us something about yourself?" Anny Beth asked.

A. J. narrowed her eyes. "Are you negotiating here?"

Melly wondered how long they could sit there looking suspiciously at each other. She remembered a game she and her brothers and sisters had played as children when they had secrets: "I won't tell until you tell." "But I won't tell until you tell." "But I won't tell until—" They could go on for hours like that. But this was a much bigger secret than "We're having blackberry pie for supper."

"Let us sign something," Melly said. "We'll promise not to tell anyone anything about you unless you say it's okay. But please—you explain why you were trying to track me down. Then we'll know if it's okay to tell you everything."

A. J. seemed to be sizing them up. Melly tried to sit up straight and look like less of a little kid. *If she refuses,* Melly thought, *do I trust her enough to tell her the whole story anyway? She did pay our fine for us, but still. . . .*

It didn't matter. A. J. relented.

"Okay," she said finally. "It's not like anybody cares what I'm doing anyway."

Melly settled back in her chair, more relaxed.

"I was a reporter for the *Lexington Herald-News*," A. J. said. "I was doing good work. I was—I think—making a difference in the world. In public affairs. But last year it stopped mattering to me. All those corrupt politicians, all those dishonest business schemes—what did it matter if I exposed them or not? For every injustice I helped correct, another one just popped up in its place."

"Midlife crisis," Anny Beth diagnosed in a professional tone.

A. J. laughed sardonically. "Yeah, that's easy for you to say," she retorted. "Some nice, neat term makes it sound insignificant, right? Just wait until it happens to you."

Melly longed to tell her that it had. Twice. Here, finally, was someone they were going to be entirely honest with. It was hard to wait even another ten or fifteen minutes. But she mustn't ruin things by jumping the gun.

"Did you want a baby?" she asked instead, thinking of the biological clock that had waylaid her.

"I didn't know what I wanted," A. J. replied. "I kept working for about six more months, but I kept getting more and more depressed. It didn't help that I broke up with my boyfriend right about then."

"Another journalist?" Anny Beth suggested.

A. J. raised her eyebrows. "How did you know?"

"Professional guess," Anny Beth said.

A. J.'s eyebrows went higher at Anny Beth's use of the word *professional.* Her expression clearly said, "You're a teenager. How can you be a professional at anything?" She seemed about to ask out loud, but cleared her throat instead.

"Anyhow," she went on, "he and I stopped getting along, and it was probably more for professional reasons than personal ones. I just wanted to do something that really mattered. So I quit. I told everyone I was going to write a book."

"About?" Melly prompted.

"I told my Web provider it was going to be about my family." A. J. looked down at her hands. "He knew I was distantly related to both the president and Riley Standish, so I think he was expecting juicy revelations. Salacious details about their childhoods."

"But that's not what you're interested in," Anny Beth said.

A. J. gave her a spooked look. Melly hoped that Anny Beth would get the message to lay off the psychologist act.

"No," A. J. said slowly. "I'm not. But I'm really not sure anymore what I am interested in."

"Then what are you looking for?" Melly asked. "Why dig up the past?"

"I don't know," A. J. said with a misery that Melly remembered well. "I think, in the beginning, I wanted some sense of where I'd come from, so I'd know where I was going. Both my parents died when I was fairly young, so I felt . . . cut off."

"So why didn't you reconnect with all your current relatives?" Anny Beth asked. "The living ones?"

A. J. frowned. "I can find out anything I want to know about any of them just by turning on my computer. None of that information is very . . . helpful."

After a night spent reading about chest sizes, strange hobbies, devout causes, and belly button fuzz, Melly was inclined to agree.

"I have a tendency to overresearch," A. J. said. "I wanted to find out everything I could about my family several generations back, when information wasn't so plentiful. I started thinking about looking at how my ancestors had been affected by the times they'd lived in—not just wars and riots and the various rights movements, but public affairs in general."

"To convince yourself that public affairs really were important," Anny Beth said.

Melly elbowed Anny Beth in the side and hissed, "Shh!"

But now A. J. seemed too deep into her story to care that the teenager in front of her was not sounding much like a teenager.

"Maybe," she conceded. "Or maybe to convince myself that public affairs really weren't important. Because what I found was, when I went very far back in my family, they were largely unaffected. In the hills of Kentucky it was generations before civil rights or women's lib had an impact. I thought, what a great premise! I thought a book about how people can live without constant updates on the rest of civilization could be revolutionary in this day and age. I got permission from the Department of Protected Lands to move back here. I wanted to live like my ancestors had, cut off from the rest of society."

Melly and Anny Beth exchanged glances.

"Did I figure her out or what?" Melly muttered under her breath.

"Okay, fine, you can have my Ph.D. in psychology," Anny Beth muttered back.

A. J. seemed not to notice their whispering. She seemed hypnotized by her own story. "Except for research on my book, I haven't made or taken any phone calls or E-mails in six months. I've avoided all news. Occasionally I go to the Wal-Mart Universal for supplies, but those are my only outings. I've been entirely alone."

"But that's not how your ancestors lived," Melly protested. "People weren't all alone in the past. They just had smaller communities that mattered to them, that"—she tried to use the word A. J. kept focusing on—"that affected them. They were perfectly happy within their own families—"

"Speak for yourself," Anny Beth muttered.

A. J. peered at Melly with a puzzled expression. "What a novel idea," she said thoughtfully. "I'll have to think about that. Would it be possible just to focus on one small group of people?"

Anny Beth wasn't concerned about helping A. J.'s understanding of the past. "So that explains what you're doing here. But why were you looking for Amelia Hazelwood?" she asked.

"In the course of my research I found one woman who was uniquely unaffected by the events around her. My great-great-great-grandmother. All those wars in the twentieth century—but none of the men in her life went off to fight them."

Melly remembered passages from her Memory Books: *Roy came home from Jackson and said his eyesight was too bad for the infantry. Thank God! But I couldn't tell him that. He was upset. He acted like he couldn't be a real man if he wasn't going off to war . . .* And later: *Pearl Harbor Day came on Burrell's birthday, when we were all together eating cake. I remember sitting around the table, the radio on, looking around and rejoicing that all my sons were too young. I kept praying, 'Thank you, God, thank you, God, for sending us all daughters at first.'*

A. J. was still ticking off the ways that Amelia Hazelwood had been unaffected by the times she'd lived in. "I even looked at things like rural electrification—it's hard to believe, but some people in this area of the country didn't have electricity in their homes until the 1960s. And I thought that might have had an impact on Amelia Hazelwood's life. What would it be like never to turn on a light until you were in your sixties? But it turns out her husband was something of an inventor, and he wired up their home with a portable generator years earlier."

Melly was a little insulted. A. J. was making it sound like she'd lived her life in a bubble or something. Of course she'd been affected by the times she'd lived in. She didn't remember directly, of course, but her Memory Book of the year she was forty-four was filled with the grief she'd felt for the people of Dry Gulch, whose sons were all wiped out in a single Japanese raid, half a world away. And even during World War I she remembered the hurtful gossip about the one German man in town. People had said he was a spy—though what he might have spied on in their part of the state was beyond her. And so what if she'd got electricity at a different time than her neighbors? She'd still made the same transition.

Melly bit the inside of her lip to refrain from telling A. J. her whole premise was crazy. A. J. obviously didn't realize the woman she was talking about was sitting right in front of her.

"But I wanted to be absolutely sure of everything," A. J. continued. "And I got bogged down on a very routine detail: her death."

Melly felt her heartbeat quicken. Hadn't the agency faked her death well enough?

"What was strange about that?" Anny Beth asked in an amazingly calm voice.

"Nothing about the death itself, as far as I knew then," A. J. said. "She clearly died of old age. But the funeral notice that appeared in the local paper showed a different date than the death certificate."

"Doesn't sound too weird to me," Anny Beth said. "People make mistakes all the time."

Melly wondered if Anny Beth had picked up on the past tense in A. J.'s narration: "as far as I knew then." Was Anny Beth having second thoughts about trusting A. J.? Did she already know too much anyhow? And if A. J. had found the discrepancy, would anyone else?

"I wanted to be accurate," A. J. was insisting. "So I E-mailed every Hazelwood I could find to see if anyone in the world had the correct information."

"That's how I got the first E-mail," Melly muttered. "So it was innocent."

A. J. gave her a questioning look but went on. "I found one old-timer who remembered the funeral, and remembered the adults at the funeral talking about how their great-grandma had done something really wacky and donated her body to science. Something called the Agency for Studying Aging. She remembered the name only because she thought it was ridiculous to be studying aging on someone who wasn't aging anymore. I figured if this agency was anything important, I would have heard of it, but I tracked it down anyway and was stunned to discover it still existed. When I called, they stonewalled me on everything—"

"Which only made you more determined," Anny Beth guessed.

"Yeah. It seemed like they had something to hide. I accessed their address files—"

"Isn't that illegal?" Anny Beth interrupted.

"Not if they don't have them protected," A. J. defended herself. "And they didn't."

Anny Beth and Melly exchanged glances. Had the agency got sloppy? Or were the officials trying to destroy them?

"I found an Amelia Hazelwood listed as living in North Dakota. I knew it wasn't the same one, of course, but I thought there had to be a connection. I was being cautious now. I started calling neighbors but didn't get much information."

Melly grinned to herself. Thank goodness A. J. had only reached Mrs. Rodney's answering machine! And none of their other neighbors even knew them.

"But when I finally called this Amelia Hazelwood herself, I got the message that she'd moved without a forwarding address."

Melly grimaced. Curses on computers that gave out information automatically.

"So I went back to the mysterious agency's address list and found a new phone number, in New Mexico. It crossed my mind that this Amelia Hazelwood might be running from my calls, but I couldn't see it. Nobody runs from reporters' calls in this day and age. So I tried calling, with no answer. The next time I called the agency, Amelia Hazelwood was erased from their address list."

Melly wondered what that meant.

"What did you think happened?" Anny Beth asked in the same voice a teacher might use to test a student. "What did you think the connection was between the Amelia Hazelwood you were studying and the one in the agency listing?"

A. J. squinted off into the distance, looking out the window as though the answer were hidden in the forsythia bush outside.

"I was thinking clones," she finally said. "Cloning humans was illegal, even way back in the year 2000, but I thought maybe this mysterious agency had done it. People were experimenting with it then. And I've checked the agency out thoroughly since then—it mainly seems to exist in order to sabotage other people's scientific research and lobby for strange causes. That might fit in with having once dabbled in illegal science."

Melly felt weak. "You think I'm a clone?" she asked incredulously.

"No," A. J. said firmly. "Not you. You're only—what'd the police officer say? Fifteen? There might have been cloning going on eighty-four years ago, but not since then. The Bureau to Prevent Illegal Scientific Procedures has too much power in this century."

"So that makes us . . . ?" Anny Beth probed again.

A. J. shrugged. "I don't know. Two teenagers, probably too smart for their own good, who maybe hacked into my phone records and figured they could play with my mind a little. And because I've been sitting out here for weeks with no one to talk to but my dog, I fell for your ruse and spilled my guts. If I had to guess, I'd say it's just a coincidence that you're named Amelia Hazelwood. Now, are you going to try to make something up, or should I just say thanks for listening?"

Melly stood up and began heading for the door. Anny Beth looked at her in amazement.

"Where are you going?" she called after her.

"I'll be right back," Melly said. "Don't leave."

It was a struggle carrying the heavy boxes down

the hill, but when she returned, Anny Beth and A. J. were still sitting there, waiting. Melly took a Memory Book off the top of the box and handed it to A. J.

A. J. opened it and started reading aloud: "'The spring I turned sixteen I fell in love. I knew there was a war going on in Europe, and it seemed wrong, wrong, wrong that so many people were in pain and dying when I was so happy. . . .'" A. J. studied the old-fashioned script, touched the words as if doubting anything so ancient sounding could be so clear and unfaded. "Where did you find these?"

"I wrote them," Melly said simply.

And then the whole story spilled out. Anny Beth and Melly alternated in the telling, sometimes getting ahead of themselves, sometimes having to pull out the books and point to a particular passage, as if that proved their tale. About halfway through A. J.'s journalistic instincts seemed to kick in, and she began interviewing them. It was what Melly had spent a lifetime dreading—having a journalist ask in that concerned tone, "And how did you feel when . . ." But A. J.'s concern seemed real. And there were no cameras rolling, no crowds slavering for the next detail, only the quiet house around them and, beyond, the mountains Melly had missed for an entire lifetime.

Finally they'd told all they could.

"So," Anny Beth challenged, "do you believe us?"

A. J. wore a look of amazement—either at them or at herself.

"Yes," she said. "I do."

Melly gulped. "So what's it going to be?" she asked. "Are you going to get that Pulitzer in the most prestigious category, the tabloid story of the century? Or will you be our mommy when we get young?"

As soon as she'd said them, Melly longed to take back her words. "Will you be our mommy. . . ." Pathetic. It made her sound like a little kid already. Why hadn't she said "caretaker"? Or "guardian"? She knew—she didn't want those things. She wanted a mommy. When she was eight and five and two and an infant, that was what she would need.

Anxiously Melly watched A. J.'s reaction. She didn't speak right away. Melly wondered how she could have been so foolhardy. A. J. wasn't a mommy. She was a journalist. But a transformation was working over A. J.'s face. At first she just looked stunned, as if it had never occurred to her that Melly and Anny Beth had had such a strong reason for telling her their tale. Then she looked thoughtful. She brought her hand up to her chin and rested it there. She turned her head slightly and stared out the window. "Your mommy," she repeated softly, as if trying out the word. Melly prayed that A. J. understood what she meant.

"I think . . . ," A. J. started. Melly froze, waiting. Beside her she heard Anny Beth catch her breath. A. J. continued, "I think that would be good for all of us."

An expression crept over A. J.'s face that Melly hadn't seen there before: She looked purposeful.

She wasn't just wandering around in old records, trying to figure out how it related to her life and if it could become a book. She had a mission now. She had a reason to live for someone besides herself.

Melly heard Anny Beth exhale sharply.

"Really?" she said. "Hot dog!" She punched Melly in the arm. "There! Are you finally satisfied?"

Melly laughed, giddy all of a sudden. "Yes," she said. "I am."

And then none of them knew what to do.

"Do I start now?" A. J. asked. "Am I supposed to ask you questions like, 'Did you wipe your feet when you came in?' 'Are you getting enough vegetables to eat?'"

"No," Anny Beth said sharply. "You're not raising us. It's more like . . . lowering us."

Melly wished Anny Beth had chosen a different word. *Lowering* reminded her of coffins being eased into a grave. She remembered all the gallows humor that had gone on in their early days at the agency—a carryover from the nursing home, when they all still assumed they were close to death. Were those kinds of jokes going to be part of her second childhood, as she slipped toward death?

"You know," A. J. said thoughtfully, "if you want me to take this seriously, if you want me to really do the best I can to take care of you, I'm going to have to confront the agency and get some more information from them. They've got to be hiding something."

Melly remembered the accounts she'd written of her time in the nursing home, when she'd given up all power over her life. She had no intention of letting that happen again, even if she did want a mommy.

"Believe me, they've told us more than we want to know," she said bitterly.

"But let me get this straight," A. J. said. "They say after you work back to being a newborn baby, on your birthday you just die? And they can't stop it?"

"That's what Dr. Reed and Dr. Jimson hypothesized all those years ago when the Cure kept failing. Melly and I were the two oldest people to receive the Turnabout injection, so it's probably happened to some of the others already. Nobody's told us otherwise," Anny Beth explained.

A. J. just looked from Anny Beth to Melly and back again.

"Okay, okay!" Melly relented. "Find out whatever you want."

"Will you two go back to the agency with me?" A. J. asked. "I'll need your help. I promise—I won't let them keep you there."

Melly waited for Anny Beth to come out with her usual, "Absolutely not! I'm not stepping foot in that place ever again!" It didn't come. Melly was ready to give her own refusal, but then she stopped. Somehow, with A. J., it might be all right to go back to the agency. It wouldn't be like they belonged at the agency. They'd belong with A. J.

"You don't have to answer right away," A. J. said. "I think finding a long-lost descendant, facing the police, getting a commitment of parenthood, and telling your stories for the first time in eighty-four years is enough for one morning. Now that I'm a mommy," she teased, "I have to insist we go have lunch."

Her pronouncement coincided exactly with the donging of the big grandfather's clock in the hall. They all laughed, and the tension dispelled. Melly decided she would like living with A. J. But they couldn't hide out in Kentucky forever. They'd have to face the agency once more.

May 15, 2085

The long driveway curved ahead of them.

"Anything look familiar yet?" A. J. asked as she programmed the car to slow down.

"Don't know," Anny Beth replied tersely. "We mainly saw things from the inside."

Trees and grass slid by the windows. They might as well be on another nature preserve, for all the greenery around them. And then the agency's main building loomed ahead of them. Melly inhaled sharply.

"That's it!" she hollered. "Right there."

A. J. stopped the car, and they stepped out. All three of them stood still for a while. Melly recognized the fake Doric columns, the sturdy-looking brick, the green-shuttered windows. Everything seemed to be just as it'd been nearly eighty years earlier. Not that Melly remembered it that well. The day she left she'd never even looked back.

"Strange," A. J. muttered, swiveling her head to take in the entire grounds.

"What?" Melly asked nervously.

"Didn't you say you two were the oldest in Project Turnabout? Wouldn't most of the others be little kids now? Four, five, six years old?" A. J. asked.

"Yeah. So?" Anny Beth asked.

"Where's the playground? Why aren't there any toys in sight?"

Melly shivered, feeling a sense of foreboding she didn't understand.

"Believe me, the others would be the kind of geeky kids who stayed glued to the computer all day," Anny Beth said. Melly wondered if she was really as unconcerned as she sounded.

A. J. rang the doorbell, and someone buzzed them in.

The entryway was empty and felt forbidding. The lights weren't even turned on.

Anny Beth elbowed Melly. "Look."

Melly turned and saw an old-fashioned pay phone still hanging on the wall by the door. As if a voice from the past were echoing in the hallway, she remembered the taunt Anny Beth had once flung at Mrs. Swanson: "There's a pay phone in the hallway. Why don't you use it?" She wondered why it was still there. Why did this feel more like a museum than an institution for kids?

"Hello?" A. J. called.

Agatha, the receptionist Melly, Anny Beth, and A. J. had spoken with before, appeared from around a corner.

"Sorry," she said. "I was checking on some things in the back. Come right in. We're so glad to see you. We were so worried when we lost touch with you, Anny Beth and Melly."

To Melly's surprise she found herself engulfed in

a tight hug. Then Agatha threw her arms around Anny Beth, too. Melly wondered if she and Anny Beth had been too hard on the agency people all these years. Maybe they did care, even if they were misguided.

But Anny Beth, never one to be distracted by emotion, blurted out, "Where is everyone?"

"Everyone?" Agatha echoed, looking puzzled.

"All the inmates," Anny Beth said. When Agatha only looked at her blankly, she added, "I mean, the kids. The other Project Turnabout victims."

"I hope you don't think of yourself as victims," Agatha said reprovingly. But Melly noticed she didn't answer the question. Agatha's expression was now as closed as if automatic doors had swung shut across her face. "Here. Let's go into the conference room. The doctors are eager to talk to you."

She paused at the reception desk, pressed a button, and announced, "They're here." Then she led them down the hall. The room they entered wasn't the big conference room where they'd had meetings before—where Mr. Johnson had died, and Dr. Reed and Dr. Jimson had married, and Melly had realized she was forgetting the past. This room was small and nondescript, containing nothing more than a table and six chairs.

An elderly man and an elderly woman walked in, and Agatha introduced them. "Melly, Anny Beth,

A. J., I'd like you to meet Dr. Jimson-Reed-Lenoski-Yee and Dr. Jimson-Reed-Alvarez-Braun. Doctors, this is Amelia Hazelwood and Anny Beth Flick, as you know, and their great-great-great-granddaughter, A. J. Hazelwood."

Everyone shook hands. Melly judged the two doctors to be in their late fifties or early sixties, clearly aging. So here was another set of doctors who had access to PT-1, but hadn't used it.

"Well," the female doctor said. "I never expected to see the two of you back here again." There was a silence she hastened to fill. "I have to tell you how sorry we are for not doing a better job of protecting your phone numbers from public access. Because of the sensitive nature of our computer files, we've tried to handle all the data protection by ourselves. I guess this proves we're not computer experts."

"And after eighty-four years we weren't as concerned as we used to be about tabloid snooping," the male doctor added with an accusatory look at A. J. "Evidently we should have been."

A. J. looked steadily back at him. Anny Beth glared. Melly decided she should play peacemaker.

"That's all right," Melly said. "As it turned out, it was a good thing that A. J. found us. And I'm sure you'll be more careful now."

She knew they were: A. J. had checked and said she couldn't get any access to agency records at all in the past few weeks. So Melly could afford to be forgiving.

Everyone fell silent again, and Melly wondered how long Anny Beth could stand the polite tension in the air around them before she broke through with a direct question. But it wasn't Anny Beth who spoke next.

"All right," A. J. said, leaning intently across the table. "Now that that's out of the way—what else are you hiding from us that we need to know?"

The two doctors exchanged glances. Melly wondered if the hyphenated names meant that they were spouses or siblings. Regardless, that comparing look had remained in the gene pool, just as Anny Beth's directness had somehow been passed down to A. J. intact.

"It's a long story . . . ," the female doctor demurred.

"We've got all the time in the world to listen," A. J. said, undeterred.

Both doctors sighed.

"Some of it's not very pleasant," the male doctor added.

"We could have figured that out," Anny Beth said. "Now, tell it. And don't pretty it up any."

The female doctor began. "After you left, our grandparents thought they'd have the Cure figured out in a matter of years. Or, at the very least, they thought they could solve the memory problems. But both solutions eluded them, and that was . . . agonizing for the patients who remained here."

She fell silent. Now it was Melly who found the suspense unbearable. "Look, we know some of them committed suicide. Your grandparents told me thirty years ago, so you don't have to pussyfoot around that. What about the others?"

"They're all dead," the male doctor said harshly.

Melly gasped, stunned beyond words. She waited for some tide of grief to overwhelm her for the people she'd lived with eighty years ago—Mrs. Englewood, who'd sipped her tea so daintily; Mr. Wilde, who'd told stupid jokes; Mrs. Kretz, who'd always bragged about how she and her husband had been such wonderful dancers. But she'd known them all so long ago, and she'd known so clearly that she had to break with them. . . . In her mind they were already dead.

"Why?" A. J. asked softly.

The male doctor shook his head regretfully. "That's what we've spent years trying to figure out. We've analyzed their psychological profiles—what we have, from the primitive records of the early part of this century—and studied their cellular structure. If you view premature requests for the Cure as essentially suicidal in nature, none of the other subjects had any desire to keep living much past the accepted human life span of one hundred twenty years. We've concluded that humans are just not meant to live too long."

"What about us?" Anny Beth asked, with more finesse than she usually bothered with.

The male doctor shrugged. "We've studied everything about you two, as well. As you know. We have enough theories to fill multiple computer databases. But we don't know. Perhaps it would help if we could find the other two people who left and cut off all contact with the agency. We've searched for them as thoroughly as possible. Because we haven't found them, we can only assume they died as well, probably decades ago, when it was easier to die in anonymity."

"So," the female doctor explained, "given the dismal failure of this experiment, we've found it necessary to switch the focus of the agency. As long as you two are alive, we will never make the full story available to the public. But we've been working behind the scenes to prevent other efforts to extend human life span."

Melly gaped at her.

"But what about—," Anny Beth started to protest.

"We thought you were working on the Cure—," Melly said simultaneously.

Neither of the doctors would look Melly or Anny Beth in the eye.

"You have to understand," the male doctor said. "The breakthrough that cured cancer in the early 2020s could have also enabled humans to live virtually forever. We didn't have much time to stop it. And other researchers keep circling closer and closer to the solution—it's a full-time job just trying to throw them off track."

Melly's head was reeling. She looked at A. J. across the table, hoping she would go into the same interviewing mode she'd exhibited with Anny Beth and Melly, and somehow pull enough information out of the doctors to make everything make sense. But A. J. sprang back from the table, her eyes flashing with outrage. Melly waited for her to yell at the doctors for trying to change the entire fate of humankind based on forty-six failures. But that wasn't what she was mad about.

"So you abandoned them," she said, pointing at Melly and Anny Beth. "You changed their lives and promised to help them, and then you abandoned them. How could you? They were counting on you."

"No," Melly said quietly. "We weren't."

A. J. turned her head and looked curiously at Melly.

"That was one of the reasons we left in the first place," Melly said. "We couldn't expect the doctors at the agency to be superhuman. They were playing God, yes, but—they weren't God."

A. J. wasn't appeased. "But, having given you PT-1, they had an obligation to keep working in your interest. They should have kept working on the Cure, they should have—"

"*We* didn't give them PT-1," the male doctor interrupted. "Are we to be held responsible for our grandparents' mistakes?"

"Yes," Melly said. "And no. You apparently feel responsible enough that you've devoted yourself to their cause." She thought it horribly sad, suddenly, these two old people working in this forgotten place. How much of their lives had they given to the agency?

A. J. had more immediate concerns.

"But when Melly and Anny Beth regress back to infancy, are you going to be there for them?" A. J. argued. "Are you going to be there to help them when they lose the ability to read, to walk, to talk?"

"We're willing to, yes," the female doctor said. "But they've been quite vocal in resisting our intervention up until now. In fact, I believe that's the whole reason they've involved you in this, to avoid depending on us. Are you going to be there to help?"

A. J. looked from Anny Beth to Melly.

"Yes," she said with the ringing certainty that Melly had heard in people's voices at wedding ceremonies, at baptisms, in court. "I will."

Anny Beth cleared her throat.

"Maybe I'm missing something," she said with a touch of the Kentucky drawl that came back into her voice, it seemed, when Melly most needed to hear it. "But tell me if I've figured this right. If all the others are dead, then no one has unaged back to the beginning. So all this talk of us going back to being babies—it's all just guesses, right? And even that notion of us dying when we hit zero—you don't know for sure that's going to happen, right?"

"Right," the doctors said together.

"So we could die, we could stay infants forever, we could—who knows—start aging again?"

"Like touching base and turning around?" Melly offered.

"Maybe," the female doctor said doubtfully. "All the lab subjects our grandparents used—before animal testing was outlawed, of course—all of them died at zero."

"But the mice and rats and monkeys also stopped unaging with the Cure," the male doctor added. "So correlations aren't . . . perfect."

"You've got to start working on this again," A. J. said threateningly. "Melly's only got another fifteen years. Before she gets back to zero, you've got to find some way to help. And you've got to let us know what you're doing—"

"No." Melly shook her head slowly. "I don't want to spend the rest of my life worrying about that. But I'm not sure you should keep messing up other people's research."

"What?" the male doctor asked in surprise.

"Think about who your grandparents picked for Project Turnabout. We were all ready to die. Cheating death was more confusing for us than joyous. And then, for practical reasons, we all agreed to be cut off from the people who meant the most to us. . . . What if they'd given PT-1 to a bunch who were fighting to live, who had people and causes to live for?"

The two doctors looked at each other thoughtfully.

"But why did you two want to live when the others didn't?" the female doctor asked. "You were as close to death as any of them."

Melly frowned. It was hard to analyze her own motives, especially since they'd changed over the years. She tried to think of something that had been constant throughout her entire second lifetime. And then she had it.

"I think I was just determined to prove that I could make it outside the agency," she said. "During my first lifetime I'd just done what people told me to do, been who they expected me to be. Once I realized I had another life coming, I had to prove I could meet the challenge."

Anny Beth nodded. "And I had such a bad life the first time, I had to prove I could manage not to mess up again," she said.

A. J. tilted her head thoughtfully to the side. "It's going to be real interesting living with you two," she said.

The doctors were looking horrified.

"So we've been wrong all these years?" the female doctor asked. "You think we should offer PT-1 to just . . . just anyone who wants it? Voluntarily?"

"Why not?" Anny Beth asked. "As long as they knew the risks."

The male doctor buried his face in his hands. "My life's work," he mumbled.

Melly felt a surge of sympathy. She knew how hard it was to give up ideas that had lasted a lifetime. She hurried to console him. "Maybe you haven't been all wrong. In the early part of the century, with all the overpopulation problems, PT-1 would have been very bad for society. But now— don't you think people would be less self-obsessed if they had a longer time to live? If they weren't scrambling to make their mark on the world before they'd gained any wisdom about what kind of mark to leave?"

"We'll . . . we'll have to think about all of this," the female doctor said.

"Can we go home now?" Anny Beth asked. "There's a cool trail we'd like to hike this afternoon, and poky old Melly over there always wants to be in bed in time to get up and see the sunrise the next day. . . ."

"Sure," the male doctor said. "Just—you'll stay in touch, won't you?"

They all shook hands, a strangely formal ending to their meeting. As they walked out to the car A. J. shook her head.

"That was not at all the way I expected things to go," she said. "I was ready to scream and yell about getting them to tell us everything, and not letting them keep you there. I had the president's office number programmed in on the portable in my purse, in case I had to bring in the heavy hitters—"

Melly stopped short, in horror. "So you would have blown our cover."

A. J. put a steadying hand on her shoulder. "Good grief, no. Don't you think the president of the United States is capable of secrecy? You guys have seen the public face of this society. But believe me, there's more. And we're going to live in secret for the next two decades."

Melly turned and faced her. "Is that really okay with you?"

A. J. nodded. "It's what I want. I swear. On the graves of my ancestors. At least—the ones who are really dead. That I know of."

They all laughed.

They got into the car and leaned back in comfort.

It would only be a couple hours to home.

"But I've got to ask you," A. J. said suddenly. "How can you stand not knowing what's going to happen at the end, when you turn zero? How can you not be grabbing those doctors by the collars and begging them to find out for you?"

Melly shrugged. "Life's full of uncertainty. Whether you're aging or unaging."

Anny Beth nodded her agreement.

A. J. squinted over at them. "I never know with you two—is that teenage profundity or the wisdom of two lifetimes?"

"How am I supposed to know?" Melly said. "It's just something I thought."

They reached the crest of the hill, and then the entire valley lay at their feet—the vista Melly had been longing to see again for her entire second lifetime.

"So," Anny Beth asked, "was it worth the wait?"

With tears in her eyes, Melly nodded. She looked out over the acres of treetops and took a deep breath of the cool mountain air. They'd been living with A. J. for a month now and had been back from the agency for two weeks, but Melly had held off on making this hike until exactly the right time.

"It has to be in June," she'd told Anny Beth and A. J. "That's when we used to go there picking blueberries. . . . That's when it'll be at its best. . . ."

Now she stood peering out at the valley in silence. It was beautiful, and yet—

A. J. puffed up the trail behind them.

"I'm going to have to get some of that PT-1 just to keep up with you two," she joked. "Could you have stopped running for a few minutes to save my pride?"

"Would you ever take PT-1?" Melly asked quietly.

"I don't know," A. J. said, just as seriously. "What do you two think?"

"I think it's a personal decision that every human will have to make for him- or herself, according to the guidance of his or her conscience, and God, if he or she so believes," Anny Beth said jauntily, as if quoting from a manual.

"Gee, thanks for the psychobabble," A. J. said. She bent over, panting, then looked out at the view. "Wow," she said. "I know it's inadequate, but, wow. No wonder you wanted to come back here."

The tears began sliding down Melly's face.

"Memories?" A. J. asked gently.

Melly wiped the tears away with the back of her hand. "No. I mean—yes, there are lots of memories. It seems like memories are always most vivid right before I lose them. And I came here a lot the summer I was fifteen. Me and Roy. . . . But that's not why I'm crying. It's because . . . because I feel old again."

"What?" A. J. asked. "After the way you charged up that mountainside?" She looked from Melly to Anny Beth and back again. "Is it just because the memories seem so long ago?"

"No," Melly said impatiently. "It's because—" She stopped.

"I think I know what you mean," Anny Beth said. "It's that—" But she couldn't finish either.

Frowning, A. J. shook her head. "You two are going to have to help me out here. I don't have a clue what you're talking about." She leaned against a tree trunk and waited.

"When I wanted to come here all those years

ago—when I wanted to have a baby . . . ," Melly started slowly. "I was looking for something. Not just scenery. I wanted to find a . . . a purpose for my life. And now—"

"What?" A. J. asked.

"Now I don't need one anymore. Everything's settled. We found you. I'm just waiting to die again."

A. J. kicked at some leaves on the ground. "You don't know that," she said. "Whatever happened to 'life's full of uncertainty'? You might do another turnabout, in which case you'd have another whole life to live—"

"But why?" Melly said. "What would the purpose of that be?"

"You found purpose in this lifetime. Surely you could do that again," A. J. said. But she didn't sound very sure of herself.

"Maybe," Melly said doubtfully. "When I was an adult again. But now there's nothing I'm supposed to do. Before, when I was a teacher and a nurse and everything else, I had a reason for living. And even just a couple months ago we were trying to outsmart the agency, and trying to find someone to take care of us. But now—we're just playing. Entertaining ourselves. Taking hikes, having picnics . . ."

A. J. nodded, finally seeming to understand. "I have some ideas of things for you to do," she said.

"What?" Melly asked eagerly.

"I think the agency needs some advice. I think society needs some advice. If the agency really is going to make PT-1 available, or at least its research available, there are going to be all sorts of ethics boards meeting and discussing what this means for society and what humanity should do about it. They may decide to ban PT-1 the way they banned cloning. They may decide to give it to everyone. Either way they'd make a better decision if you two shared your experiences."

Anny Beth and Melly stared at her in dismay, utterly speechless. Anny Beth was the first one to regain her voice.

"But you promised us privacy!" Anny Beth protested. "We'd make spectacles of ourselves. We'd be just like all those bozos with their own twenty-four-hour video broadcasts, telling the world every thought that crossed our minds—"

"No," A. J. said. "Neither of you would be like that. You'd be thoughtful and wise and reveal only what needed to be revealed. You could teach our whole society the difference between openness and exhibitionism."

"We've spent eighty-four years trying to avoid being exposed. And now you want us to tell our stories? Just like that?" Melly asked.

"You ran halfway across the country trying to avoid me, and then you sought me out. You promised

Dr. Reed you'd never come to Kentucky, and then you did. You gave up your families, and then you took them back. You vowed you'd never return to the agency, but then you did," A. J. said. "Shall I go on?"

It made Melly dizzy thinking about all the turnabouts she'd made in the past few weeks. A. J. made her and Anny Beth sound as reversible as, well, teenagers, trying on a different image or philosophy every other day. But it wasn't that. She remembered Anny Beth saying out in the desert, "You live long enough, you're bound to have to eat your words one time or another."

A. J. continued, speaking more softly. "You guys haven't lived your lives scandalously enough to keep the interest of the tabloid media for long. If you went forward and spoke out about PT-1, there would be a buzz for a week or so, but then you'd be left alone. They'd go on to the next hyped event du jour. And you could take part in the serious discussion of what this really means for humanity."

Melly bit her lip and looked back out at the sky and trees. "I'll—" She looked at Anny Beth. "We'll think about it."

"Oh, great," Anny Beth grumbled. "Do you feel better? Making me think—always having to have some purpose." She turned and shouted out at the scenery, "I just want to have fun."

The words echoed: "—fun . . . fun . . . fun." But Anny Beth grinned and nodded at Melly when she turned around.

"Reckon we could try our hands at writing a book or something," she said. "Maybe we could even do it anonymously, avoid the tabloids entirely. You think?"

Melly thought how strange Anny Beth's suggestion would have sounded to her the last time she was fifteen. How could she, Amelia Hazelwood, write a book? But now—A. J. was right. She did have things to say. She had a purpose again.

Impulsively Melly threw her arms around Anny Beth's neck, then included A. J. in the hug too.

"What a family," A. J. said, laughing.

For a long time the three of them stood on the edge of the precipice, looking out as far as they could see.

Then, "Race you down the hill?" Anny Beth asked.

For an answer Melly took off running, wind in her hair, pulse pounding in her ears, a clear path ahead of her.

Clear, at least, until the next bend in the road.

Author's Note

I picked a fairly obscure scientific theory to explain the unaging in *Turnabout*. So I was stunned when that theory began making headlines before I'd even finished writing the book.

Though I didn't exactly toe the line scientifically in this book, the telomeres that Dr. Reed raves about during Project Turnabout aren't fiction. They do exist, and they are indeed like beads on a necklace. They're repeating sequences of genetic material on the ends of chromosomes. (I realize I probably just lost everybody who didn't cram for some sort of genetics exam within the past twenty-four hours. To explain: Chromosomes are chains of genes, linked in pairs in the nuclei in your body's cells. It's like having a recipe for everything about you in every cell in your body.)

Telomeres don't have any direct impact on, say, what color your eyes are or how tall you grow, the way other parts of your chromosomes do. Some scientists compare telomeres to the plastic tips of shoelaces—they keep the shoelaces from unraveling. But in most normal human cells, every time the cell reproduces, the telomeres get shorter. If you don't like the necklace or shoelace analogy, you can think of it this way: It's like making a photocopy on a copy machine with a shrinking screen—every time you make a copy, part of the copy gets cut off. As long as the telomeres are there, it's not that big a deal to lose part of the copy, because the telomeres protect the important stuff. They function like a nonessential frame.

Until you run out of frame, and the copier starts losing part of the picture.

With an explanation like that it's easy to jump to conclusions—when your cells are almost out of telomeres, you get old. And when they're gone, you die, right?

Sorry. It's not nearly that simple.

If you're really interested in the science behind all this, I'll explain. If you're just curious about whether you or your friends or your parents or your great-aunt Enid will ever unage, skip ahead a few paragraphs. I'll get past the technical stuff. I promise.

Back in 1961 a researcher named Leonard Hayflick discovered that normal human cells in test tubes divide about fifty times and then die. The Hayflick Limit appeared ironclad: If you take cells that have divided twenty times and stick them in the freezer for a year, when they thaw, they divide about thirty more times and then die. In contrast to cancer cells, which can reproduce endlessly, normal cells clearly had some sort of internal clock telling them when to die.

About a decade later a Russian scientist, Alexey Olovnikov, suggested that the shortening telomeres just might be that internal clock. But the scientific world didn't embrace the idea immediately. Part of the problem was the old chicken-and-egg question: Which comes first? Scientists weren't sure whether the shorter telomeres caused the cells to age and die, or whether the cells aging and dying caused the shorter telomeres.

But in January 1998, when I was about halfway through writing this book, researchers at the University of Texas Southwestern Medical Center in Dallas, and Geron Corporation in Menlo Park, California, announced that they had figured out how to restore telomeres—preventing the cells from dying. Using an enzyme called telomerase, they allowed otherwise normal cells to divide many times past the Hayflick Limit.

The headline for the *USA Today* story about the announcement proclaimed, 'FOUNTAIN OF YOUTH' FOR CELLS DISCOVERED.

I was more than a little freaked out by the notion that my book might be obsolete before it was even published.

But the 1998 announcement just concerned cells in a test tube, a far cry from experiments on elderly people in nursing homes. Also, some scientists worried that the telomerase might cause normal cells to begin acting like cancer cells. After all, it's telomerase that some cancer cells use to stay immortal.

And many questions remain about translating test tube results to real humans. The relationship between cells living and dying, and humans living and dying, is still not completely clear. Just to give one example: The cells of the brain and heart—certainly two of our most important organs—stop dividing in youth. So how could telomere loss be blamed when brains and hearts age and die?

As I write this, research continues. The Geron Corporation scientists are hoping their work will lead to "therapeutic opportunities for age-related diseases," according to the *New York Times.* As far as I know, no one is expecting to produce anything like PT-1, if that's even possible. Although some observers hype the potential for immortality, most scientists are looking at narrower changes: combating cancer, treating hardened arteries, growing new skin for burn victims, reversing vision loss, eliminating wrinkles. For the foreseeable future, at least, people will still die—the telomere research might just help them live longer and stay healthier before death.

So your great-aunt Enid's chances for complete unaging look pretty slim. Your parents' odds aren't much better. But will people who are kids today ever face the kind of decisions Melly and Anny Beth faced?

Beats me.

Would you want to?

Lia Kahn was perfect: rich, beautiful, popular.

Until the accident that nearly killed her.

Now she has been downloaded into a new body that only looks human.

Lia will never feel pain again, she will never age, and she can't ever truly die.

But some miracles come at a price. . . .

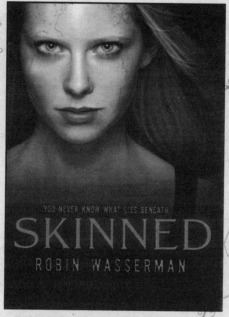

THE FIRST BOOK IN A GRIPPING TRILOGY

"A spellbinding story about loss, rebirth,
and finding out who we really are inside.
This intense and moving novel will wind up under your skin."
—SCOTT WESTERFELD

New York Times bestselling author of the Uglies series

From Simon Pulse | Published by Simon & Schuster

**A girl who can enter other people's dreams.
A gift that feels like a curse.**

Wake

Fade

From Simon Pulse
PUBLISHED BY SIMON & SCHUSTER

MARGARET PETERSON HADDIX is the author of many memorable novels for young readers, including *Just Ella, Among the Hidden,* and *Running Out of Time.* Her work has been honored with the International Reading Association Children's Book Award, American Library Association Best Books for Young Adults and Quick Pick for Reluctant Young Adult Readers citations, and several state readers' choice awards. Margaret graduated from Miami University with degrees in creative writing, journalism, and history, and has worked as a newspaper reporter and a community college instructor. She lives in Columbus, Ohio, with her husband, Doug, and their children, Meredith and Connor.

Where did the idea for *Turnabout* come from? "I bought a card for a friend, joking that it's actually good that we get older, not younger, on our birthdays because—as the punch line went—who would want to live through puberty twice? It made me wonder: What if someone had to? I already had age and aging on my mind because I'd just attended my grandmother's ninetieth birthday party, and I'd recently visited my husband's grandmother in Kentucky, a month before her death. Somehow all those things—the card's question, the ninetieth birthday, the Kentucky visit—meshed in my mind. *Turnabout* was the result."